Tethers

An addictively charming romantic suspense.

Rachael Broadhurst

First published in Great Britain in 2024

Copyright © Rachael Broadhurst 2024

Rachael Broadhurst asserts the moral right to be identified as the author of this work in accordance with the Copyright Designs and Patents Act, 1988.

All rights reserved.

No part of this publication may be reproduced, distributed, or transmitted in any form or by any means, including photocopying, recording, or other electronic or mechanical methods without the prior written permission of the author.

ISBN: 979-8-8793-7212-0

001

This book is sold subject to the condition that it shall not, by way of trade or otherwise, be lent, re-sold, hired out, or otherwise circulated without the copyright holder's prior consent in any form of binding or cover other than that in which it is published and without a similar condition including this condition being imposed on the subsequent purchaser.

Edited by Simon Persey, UK
Formatted by UK Design Co. – www.ukdesigncompany.co.uk
Assistant Editor: David Amos

Tethers

Chapter One

From this height, the mud hut in which Fleur had purchased her ticket resembled a molehill. As she continued to ascend, her recently-escaped past seemed more distant still.

Fleur let go of the harness mildly compressing her ribcage and outstretched her arms. She studied the sky - the top half was the royal blue of the closing day, the bottom half the vivid pinks and purples of impending night. The sun had all but disappeared behind the African ocean. Fleur floated forwards, gaining speed with the wind, gently chasing the remaining rays. There was nothing below her but the water. The feeling was at once unusual and supremely beautiful; she was flying.

The neighbouring island of São Pedro looked exquisite on the horizon. Sleepy silhouettes reclined on white-sand beaches, perfectly anonymous amidst the low clouds. A blanket of shadow slowly buried the scene in all the deeper colours of night.

Fleur's chest jerked painfully, she let out a yelp. The rope tethering her to the ground had reached its full extension. The five ginormous balloons suspending her bumped clumsily into one another, generating their own noisy protest overhead. Fleur massaged her limbs as the lingering discomfort pulsed

Chapter One

deeply throughout her body.

She would now have to be, quite literally, dragged back down to earth. Three large men on the cliff got to work. They grabbed the line and yanked in unison, reeling Fleur in with harsh bursts of synchronised force.

Despite the obvious landing issues faced by *Moses' Magical Balloon Experience* (not to mention the questionable name), the tourist attraction suited Fleur immeasurably.

* * *

Six small buildings comprised Moses' premises - huts, shacks and (at odds with the surroundings) a newly-erected concrete structure. Moses had claimed the latter for his office, although he generously granted his workers use of the lockers located inside.

The 'Staff Shed' was illuminated by a single hanging bulb. White light painted the wooden interior in stark strokes. There was no flooring underfoot. Fleur curled her toes, collecting sand in the creases. She was unsure why Moses had insisted upon the removal of her shoes prior to entry.

"I work at the hotel but two jobs is okay," Fleur simplified her language, sliding the 'Worker Wanted' flyer from her cardigan pocket. "How many days of the week do you want me?"

"Three half-of-days," Moses spoke in broken English, the accent was hard to place. "Twenty euro per shift payment."

Tethers by Rachael Broadhurst

Fleur pondered his offer. The walls soon filled the silence, creaking as they tilted with the breeze.

"This will be staff room for you," Moses provided a poor selling point.

Fleur spotted a poster on the door. It showed an airborne teenager giving a thumbs-up, with balloons on long wires attached to his harness - the same equipment from which Fleur had been so recently released. Her ribs were still aching from the activity.

She watched the adolescent rock slowly back and forth with the building.

"I've never seen anything like this place! It's definitely safe?"

"Of course," Moses said, beaming with pride, "three years of business, zero death."

Fleur held back a laugh.

He continued unaware, "Customer fly up, he come back down. No problem!"

Moses paused, considering his audience.

"My staff take flight any time, no charge."

Although Fleur deemed 'flight' to be a strong word for Moses' services, she extended a hand in acceptance of her new employment. Moses wrapped her instead in a suffocating bear hug.

Chapter One

"Welcome to the team!"

Fleur smiled through her aversion to physical contact.

Tethers by Rachael Broadhurst

Eric and Caroline

It was nearly three o'clock in the morning. The couple were unknowingly enjoying their last few moments of sleep. The silver clock sat smugly next to the pilot's head, ready to wreak havoc right on cue.

A piercing chorus of ringing shattered the serenity. Eric sat up and began fumbling blindly for the source of the sound, a rare lack of composure plaguing him. He flicked the switch and hushed the clanging contraption, regretting - as he did most days - his purchase of the loudest available alarm.

The fog of dreamy confusion took a little longer than normal to dissipate - it was an especially early start for the man.

"Two hours. We're leaving in two hours," Eric whispered, shaking his wife.

Caroline groaned in agreement before swiftly resuming her sleeping.

Two hours and fifteen minutes later, the pair were luggage-laden and en route to the car. The perk of worldwide travel was earned by Eric but primarily enjoyed by his wife. She frequently accompanied him on his ventures overseas and revelled in sharing their holiday tales with envious friends.

Although a regular flyer, Caroline was seldom a prepared one. She dropped and retrieved the same bag twice in quick succession. Her unzipped, knee-high boots were extremely

Chapter One

loud on the cobbles, echoes emanated from each heavy step - undoubtedly waking up neighbours. From the ankles up, the dress code was 'evening comfort'. Her hair was scooped into an improvised top-of-head arrangement, held together predominantly by tangles.

Eric, who had spent significantly longer getting ready, looked every bit the embodiment of professionalism. His uniform was meticulously well kept and obsessively ironed. His hair had been combed and styled into a flawless side part.

He unlocked his newly-purchased vehicle with a tap of the remote key in his pocket. Caroline clambered into the passenger seat, threw her luggage into the back and vowed to get changed once the car had reached the motorway.

***

The arrivals lounge at the African airport was busy and hot. Heat rose from every surface in blurry zigzags. Nobody wanted to be there, from the excessively polite staff in striped neckties to the jet-lagged passengers, arriving in their unstoppable hordes.

Heads turned towards Eric and the cabin crew as they passed. The flight attendants' small suitcases glided across the floor. Eric's team always managed somehow to leave the aeroplane last and the airport first. The sea of tourists parted to allow them the privilege.

Caroline attempted to catch her husband's attention but the

waving of a rolled-up magazine was not noticed by the pilot. She cursed under her breath, rejoining the queue from which she had hoped to be rescued.

Eric's expensive aftershave lingered in the air for a good few seconds after he had slipped out of the building, and into an already-waiting local taxi.

* * *

Fleur sat at her pop-up 'Hotel Representative' desk, which had been deliberately erected in the least visible corner of the hotel entrance lobby. The spacious ground floor was alive with numerous tourists, busying themselves with their various holidaymaker endeavours; they checked in to the reception, discussed hire cars and complained loudly about their sunburn.

Fleur's head rocked back and forth, as she drifted between falling asleep and waking up again. She defeatedly made a pillow out of folded arms. The room faded to blur, then quickly back to black.

"Which is the pilot's room?" a deep voice startled her bolt upright, "Eric Ryang, flight 692."

Fleur fumbled with a tiny notepad and avoided eye contact.

"Welcome to Boa Island, sir."

She found the page.

Chapter One

"You're in Suite 306," Fleur said, taking a fold-out map from the drawer. She opened it and attempted to circle the location with a biro. It took a few laps before any ink was released. "Shall I show you to reception so you can check in?"

Eric glanced at the very nearby reception.

"There's a queue."

Fleur sighed.

"But my system takes much longer!"

Eric took a second to digest the complaint.

"I can only apologise."

Fleur fired up her laptop. Although the words 'Happy to Help' were displayed on her stall, they were rarely an accurate description of her attitude. She harboured a gentle resentment towards the majority of the hotel's guests, for a large number of relatively small shortcomings.

The pilot, however, had committed a cardinal sin. Causing botheration to the hotel representative for matters better suited to reception was, in Fleur's mind, the holy grail of all misdemeanours.

She looked up. The tall man looming over her was a simultaneously impressive and imposing prospect. His stance was strong and deliberate, his gaze unblinking. Fleur felt that the potentially-desirable fullness of his lips was let down tremendously by the cold tone escaping them.

Tethers by Rachael Broadhurst

"Are we done?" he asked with a shrug.

"Don't worry, sir. I can do the rest."

Fleur managed an unconvincing smile, although her eyes were still frowning.

"It should only take me thirty minutes. Please, go and enjoy your beautiful suite."

Chapter Two

The ceiling of the burnt-orange hotel room was low, lending a boxy and claustrophobic feeling to Fleur's living quarters. The air conditioning only worked on some days and this particularly stuffy Thursday was not one of them. A wooden table was swamped with sketches, notes from meetings and crumpled customer receipts.

Fleur sat at her desk, leafing through a flyer for *Moses' Magical Balloon Experience*. The name of the attraction made her smirk a little as she studied the sun-bleached pages. She recalled her own flight with Moses, closing her eyes and feeling weightless once more as the memory lifted her, for a short time, from the gloomy surroundings. She would have given anything to soar again; the majority of her time off from the hotel seemed a small price to pay.

Fleur's current job was exhausting. It had only been three weeks since her first shift but it felt closer to an eternity. The duties were exceptionally unchallenging and the hours near-punishing.

Her thoughts lingered on her acceptance of additional employment with Moses, her mind a tornado of excitement and regret.

Tethers by Rachael Broadhurst

* * *

The hotel's karaoke night was under way. Dozens of lines of outdoor seating stretched to the back of the huge courtyard, where guests who were anxious to avoid performing tended to congregate. The front three rows were filled with very enthusiastic revellers - applauding, singing along and nervously awaiting the announcement of their name between numbers.

Fleur sat in the middle of the front row, visibly upset at having to be there.

As the intoxicated tourist on stage held his last note, Fleur darted up the steps to join him. She carefully retrieved the microphone, making great effort not to touch the man himself. The wet patch on the front of his shirt made her feel uncomfortable.

"Fantastic performance, Gary. Thank you!" she exclaimed to the crowd, watching Gary to ensure his safe descent of the stairs.

"Next up, we have," Fleur rummaged through a small, red bag and uncurled a ball of paper, "Joan!"

The silhouette of an elderly woman shuffled its way forwards. Fleur glanced at Henry, the evening's DJ, as he scoured his computer for the correct track. She found it amusing that Henry should be working in this capacity - his official title at the hotel was Swimming Pool Aerobics Instructor (very obviously

Chapter Two

his forte). There was dead air as Joan's backing music eluded him.

Fleur was back in her seat when the song finally started up.

"SIT DOWN!" a male voice called out from behind her, "YOU'RE SPILLING THAT BEER ALL OVER EVERYONE."

The previous performer was making himself unpopular, stumbling aimlessly through the aisles. Complaints were growing louder around Gary, like someone was slowly turning up the volume knob. He sat, mocking his accusers and making obscene gestures.

"THAT ISN'T EVEN YOUR CHAIR!"

The lead heckler pushed him hard, sending a shockwave through the entire row of seated guests. In retaliation, a dazed Gary struck out! The slap to the man's cheek echoed around the entire outdoor courtyard as all other sound ceased.

Fleur leapt into action. A high-pitched ringing noise in her ears quickly replaced the silence. She darted around the seats towards the brawlers as the fight progressed onto the floor. Onlookers shouted encouragingly at the violence, throwing the occasional extra kick into the grappling.

* * *

Eric guided Caroline through the courtyard. His hands were on her upper arms, applying gentle pressure to direct her walking. He released her, pulled out a chair and studied his wife with

Tethers by Rachael Broadhurst

intense interest until she was seated at the table.

Caroline's thickly applied makeup was doing little to disguise the darkness beneath her eyes. She took short, shallow breaths. A tear fell, she brushed it from her chin.

Eric's attention was caught by a commotion near to the stage. He spotted the hotel representative, holding apart two inebriated men as they yelled at one another over her shoulder.

"Let's fly home," Caroline reclaimed her husband's focus. "Please."

* * *

Fleur took a seat in the empty, all-inclusive bar. For the first time, she was glad that the evening's karaoke event was well attended. As a waiter approached, she pointed out her choice on the cocktail menu. The fight had left Fleur shaken and she hoped that alcohol would help to restore her more relaxed demeanour.

Sip one made her wince - it was strong and overbearingly sour. Persisting with the concoction, she found that the later gulps seemed somehow less repulsive.

Fleur felt increasingly less guilty about leaving Henry the DJ to handle the revellers alone. Her newfound indifference was a suit of armour, protecting her from every unwanted emotion. There was a distinct spring in her step as she made her way

Chapter Two

back to the stage. Even the pilot did not dampen Fleur's spirits when his typically miserable face came into view.

A woman's voice could be heard, somebody was sitting opposite Eric at the table. Caroline's words were hard to catch, but the delivery was markedly pleading. Eric's eyes met Fleur's as she passed.

"Helloo!" she sang cheerfully to the couple, opting for inappropriate enthusiasm over an acknowledgment of anything untoward. She did not look back for their reactions.

It was a little reassuring that Henry had won over the crowd in Fleur's absence. He was teaching the drunken mob an aerobics lesson. The change in pace was being received wonderfully by the room.

Chapter Three

The morning sun was especially hot overhead. Tourists flocked to the repurposed hotel courtyard for the breakfast buffet, sporting bright, linen outfits and unflattering tan lines. At one table, pot-bellied men loudly sang the praises of the unlimited beer tap at the juice station.

Fleur struggled to construct her stall in the stuffiest, most-hidden corner of the chaos. She wrestled with the complicated, metal skeleton.

"Excuse me?"

A woman's hand landed on her arm, causing her to jump.

"Are you okay?" Fleur felt compelled to ask, noticing that tears were dropping from behind the oversized sunglasses.

"I'm the pilot's wife," Caroline ignored the question, speaking with surprising composure. "We came in yesterday, flight 692."

She lifted the frames and patted her eyes with a tissue.

"I need to leave today."

Fleur knew that the request would be impossible to fulfil. Flights to and from Boa Island were extremely limited. It was not uncommon for pilots to spend seven nights in the hotel,

Chapter Three

along with their passengers, before making the return journey on the same aeroplane.

"I'm afraid there won't be a flight to England until tomorrow afternoon. There's a six thirty to Glasgow tonight if -"

"Tomorrow is fine," Caroline interrupted.

Fleur picked up her laptop and entered the request. The blue outline of a circle whirled on the screen as the machine searched its database. The outdated device seemed to be running even more slowly than usual.

"Will your husband be leaving too?" Fleur asked dutifully, although she had a strange feeling that the question was insensitive.

"No," Caroline replied.

* * *

"After you put harness on customer," Moses instructed, "tug strap, very hard."

He pulled at his own equipment to demonstrate, the material tightened.

"Clip tether rope, like this."

He pushed the carabiner to a large, silver ring on his chest. The metal clicked into position. Fleur nodded her understanding.

"Only attach these," Moses gestured to the balloons, "after

tourist is clip to rope. If not, he fly up!"

Moses lifted his pointed index finger to the sky, mimicking a holidaymaker's journey to the heavens.

After another hour of somewhat strange training, Fleur was ascending once more. She closed her eyes and breathed deeply, attempting - but not remotely managing - to tune out any awareness of the painful jerk soon to afflict her middle. She reached her arms forwards and wiggled her fingers, enjoying the slight resistance of the afternoon air.

The heat from the sun was sublime as it bounced off of her skin, gently staining her exposed limbs in a golden hue.

* * *

Fleur tiptoed towards her room. The overhead lighting emitted a quiet hum as it bathed the hotel entrance lobby in soft, yellow tones.

Once outside of her door, it took Fleur a short while to rescue the key from her pocket (it had been drowning in a small river of rubbish).

The evening peace was pierced by irregular clicks of high heeled shoes. Fleur turned around and saw the pilot's wife approaching with haste. A blanket covered her arms.

"Where's the pharmacy?" Caroline's breathing was erratic. "Last time I was here, it was -"

Chapter Three

"It's over there," Fleur pointed to an illuminated green cross on the opposite end of the forecourt. Her eyes widened. "Are you bleeding?"

Caroline glanced at her exposed wrist and quickly re-covered it.

"No."

Fleur stepped forwards.

"Let me see. Where's your husband?"

Caroline was already moving away, her steps distinctly clumsy on the pristinely-polished marble floor.

* * *

Dear Sarah,
What a shame it is that this beautiful paper is
filled only with my ugliest thoughts.
I'm worried about a lady in the hotel.
The pilot is so reminiscent of Daniel.

Fleur turned everything over in her mind, spinning her pen in rhythm.

"I wish someone had checked up on me," she addressed the empty room.

* * *

Fleur's determination wavered tremendously during her

journey through the huge hotel complex, her pace gradually slowing from a run to a moderately fast walk.

As she snuck towards Suite 306, she questioned her own sanity for coming at all. Her head thumped with heartbeats as she considered her next move.

Suddenly, there was an almighty crash from behind the wall! The sound echoed down the corridor and seemed to shake the entire third floor underfoot. Fleur did not hesitate, pounding the door four times with both fists.

There was a tense period of quiet before it shifted open. Caroline fought to catch her breath as she observed Fleur through the crack.

"Can I help you?"

"What was that sound?!" Fleur snapped.

"S-some furniture fell over," Caroline stuttered.

"Are you hurt?"

Caroline shook her head. Fleur checked the woman's bare arms for blood, and was mildly relieved to find none.

"Where's your husband?" she pressed.

The silence that ensued was deafening.

"You don't need to protect him," Fleur said, her eyes pleading. "Is he hurting you?"

No response.

Chapter Three

With frantic force, Fleur threw herself at the door, bursting into the suite! Caroline stumbled backwards, dazed by the impact of the wood.

Fleur scanned the room. There was no sign of Eric. Before Caroline could protest, she was running towards the bedchamber in the far corner.

"I'M SORRY," Fleur yelled behind her, "BUT I WON'T LET YOU HIDE HIM FROM ME!"

She entered.

The dimly lit room was a painting of disarray, from a garish orange palette. Dust lingered in a dense cloud over the fallen wardrobe, making the air around it hard to breathe. The wide curtain drooped, clinging to just two of the numerous hooks on the pole. Ceramic lamps were shattered, their sharp debris forming an assault course on the stone floor.

The door behind Fleur slammed shut. The key turned in the lock.

She spun.

Eric's silhouette was unmistakable.

Chapter Four

"Sir," Fleur spoke with forced confidence, "you need to accompany me to reception."

Eric did not move.

"It's not safe for you here," he said.

Fleur could feel her whole body trembling.

The pilot took a few steps forwards. As he became illuminated by the last remaining lamp in the bedchamber, Fleur's overwhelming fear was quickly replaced with cold dread. Wherever Eric's skin was visible, there were injuries. His bandaged fist hung by his side, his right eye was swollen, his bottom lip split.

Fleur instinctively paced in his direction, avoiding the shards underfoot.

"What happened?"

She pulled back the blood-soaked sleeve.

Eric whispered, "It's under control."

Fleur unravelled the shoddily-applied bandage. She gasped at the laceration across his palm.

Chapter Four

"You need to go to the hospital."

The door handle bowed as Caroline attempted to enter. She hit the wood from the other side with frustration. Fleur felt a tingling of fear travel the length of her spine.

"You need to leave," Eric warned.

Fleur noticed an open first aid kit on the table. Trying desperately to recall her recent training, she rummaged through its contents.

"ERIC?" Caroline called out from the lounge.

"Grip this," Fleur instructed, presenting a spool of bandage.

Eric took the material and squeezed tightly, wincing with the pain of the pressure. Fleur wrapped a fresh dressing around his closed fist.

"Listen," Eric stared at the door, "don't unlock it."

His eyes were wide open, his expression turning Fleur's blood cold.

"Sir, you're scaring me."

He faced her.

"Does she still have the knife?"

There was another loud thump. The thin wall rippled and shook next to them. With sudden, panic-induced determination, Fleur darted across the room.

Tethers by Rachael Broadhurst

"Follow me!"

She slid away the limp curtain, flicked the latches of the huge window and pushed the glass away from her. She assessed the low rooftops below, mapping a potential journey to the ground. Fleur realised that Eric was not behind her.

"I can't leave," he uttered, "you don't understand."

"You can," Fleur walked towards him and outstretched her hand, "and I do."

***

Eric held his bandaged fist to his chest and climbed outside. Fleur considered the jump ahead of them.

"Are you ready?"

He nodded.

Fleur hesitated for a second before launching into the air. It wasn't long before her feet loudly hit the platform below, with Eric's landing behind shortly after. The pair sprinted the length of the rooftop. They halted at the edge to assess the larger, more daunting drop that they now faced.

The descent to the next level had appeared infinitely more manageable from Fleur's earlier vantage point. The uncertainty that she felt was intensified by the absence of any immediate lighting. Before they could dwell any longer, there was another thunderous crash from Suite 306. They jumped

Chapter Four

in unison into the darkness.

Fleur cried out with the impact; pain travelled from her heel through her entire leg in one swift, hot motion.

"Are you okay?" Eric asked, looking at Fleur although it was too dark to make out her features.

"NO!" she knelt and grabbed her ankle tightly with both hands. "Just keep going."

Eric ran to the opposite end of the rooftop and, to Fleur's bemusement, proceeded to lay his body down on the stone. His right arm draped over the building's edge and he got to work fumbling with the wall.

Fleur squinted - half with confusion, half with agony.

"What are you doing?"

Eric's hand resurfaced clutching a pink spotlight. The missing beam left a sizable gap in the multicoloured display illuminating the hotel entrance below. He hurriedly returned, falling to his knees opposite Fleur and placing the light by his side.

He held her shoe and slowly twisted it in circles.

"Does this hurt?"

She winced.

He rested his palm against the sole and pushed it hard towards her body.

Tethers by Rachael Broadhurst

"And this?"

"No."

He concluded that the bone was not broken. His thumb began to massage the troubled area. Fleur closed her eyes, breathing deeply as the pain worsened then subsided with the pressure. Eric glanced up at the window through which they had just escaped.

"We can probably stay here for a while. I don't think my wife can see us."

Fleur shrugged.

"What choice do we have? I'll call the police tomorrow."

"No!" Eric insisted, "I called them in England once. When they arrived, my wife completely twisted the story. They believed her and I was given a warning for assault. I'm sorry, I can't risk it."

Fleur felt uneasy.

"Is your wife injured now?"

"No."

"I saw her earlier. There was blood on her arm."

"It must have been mine, I have never hurt her. Do you believe me?"

There was a moment of silence before Fleur answered, "I think so."

Chapter Four

* * *

"We may be here all night," Fleur realised. She peered over at the next drop and shuddered, before taking a dramatic step back. "The cleaners can bring the ladder on their morning shift."

Eric sat cross-legged, staring into the starry night. His vision had adjusted to the darkness, he studied subtle details in the landscape - from stray animals, lurking like lice on faraway hills, to the gentle drifting of sand across nearby beaches.

"Is that an ambulance?"

Fleur followed his gaze and saw a yellow van passing through the hotel gates and heading for the entrance. She smiled with renewed hope.

"Someone must have heard your fight and called -"

"Wait," Eric said, reaching up to grip her wrist.

The automatic doors of reception had slid open, revealing a dishevelled-looking Caroline limping through the lobby. Fleur watched on in bewilderment as a paramedic ran to the pilot's sobbing wife. The man observed her left shoulder then attempted to lift the wrist, causing her to let out a piercing cry. He moved to Caroline's right side and tucked his head under her arm, supporting her as she hopped towards the back of the ambulance.

Fleur glanced down at Eric, the weight of her fresh doubt

causing her legs to feel weak. He sensed her suspicion without looking up.

"My wife dislocated her shoulder on the bedroom door," he deduced, his matter-of-fact tone juxtaposing the grimness of the subject.

"And the limp?" Fleur pressed.

Her heart was thumping, close to the surface of her chest as though about to burst through.

"She cut her foot on some glass at breakfast," he answered.

Fleur closed her eyes, quickly reliving her earlier meetings with Caroline, scouring the memories for a limp in the woman's step, second-guessing her every recollection. Eric's swollen face was shiny, white with moonlight as he turned to her.

"I'm not lying."

Heavy air surrounded the rooftop like prison walls. Fleur's cellmate felt as unfamiliar as the distant African scenery, into which the ambulance disappeared.

Chapter Five

The majority of Boa Island was untouched by modern machinery. Locals were able to navigate the vast expanses of desert using only the horizon's landmarks, and their deduction of the distances.

A taxi bounced through the baron landscape. Inside, a young woman wearing a plastic tiara and bright pink T-shirt, emblazoned with the words 'Shotgun Wedding', felt increasingly regretful about her choice of hen do location. Pregnant bride-to-be Amanda rubbed her aching back.

"I hope the hotel's not too much further."

Perched one seat along, was a man to whom she had not been formally introduced. The unknown islander passionately kissed 'Loose Lucy', an inebriated member of the party. Heat from the stranger's body uncomfortably warmed Amanda's thigh, as she made every effort to stare in the opposite direction.

In front of them, two backwards-facing chairs were occupied by Rosie and Lily, otherwise known as 'Home Early' and 'Virgin Mary' respectively. The hens' shirts matched in colour but upon each had been printed a different character assassination nickname. Home Early's head moved jerkily from side to side as she slept, drool stretching somewhat impressively from her open mouth down to her lap. Virgin Mary was extremely pale with travel sickness. She watched, through the back window, fireworks of sand bursting up from behind the tyres, breathing deeply to alleviate her nausea.

'Agent Orange' sat in the passenger seat. Her artificial tan was at least four shades darker than her natural complexion (visible only in her hairline and certain spaces between her fingers). She tapped a bare foot, stroking the recently-removed flip flops in her lap and complaining loudly about her boyfriend.

"I actually think *his* behaviour is the reason I have these issues."

The driver, her comment's recipient, spoke no English. He smiled and nodded, misreading Agent Orange's tone while making every effort to appear interested.

Amanda hated being referred to as 'Shotgun Wedding'.

"It was so annoying having to explain this phrase to everyone in the nightclub. Yes, I'm getting married because I'm knocked up. Let's tell the whole world!"

She had not previously mentioned her feelings to Agent Orange, purchaser of the shirts back in London. Amanda felt a little relieved to notice that her friend was too busy with her own ranting to hear the outburst.

The vehicle joined a dirt road. An ambulance passed at great

Chapter Five

speed, causing the car to shake. Virgin Mary groaned loudly at the disturbance, her face seeming to flash momentarily green with illness.

Two detailed Agent Orange stories later, the party arrived at the hotel. They exited the taxi and raced to the back door, forgetting to pay the driver. The small man gave chase for a good few feet; the party apologetically handed over the fare, plus a few extra euros for his trouble.

Once inside of the huge shared room, Amanda collapsed onto her luxurious bed. Both feet wobbled on the frame, freeing themselves from their faux-leather shackles - the sandals slapped the stone floor as they landed. Amanda sunk into the freshly washed covers and rolled around in the perfect comfort.

She covered her exposed ear with a pillow, attempting to drown out the incessant noise of her still-active fellow revellers.

"MANDY," Agent Orange yelled from the bathroom, "SHOTGUN WEDDING!"

"WHAT?"

"CALL RECEPTION, THERE'S PEOPLE ON THE ROOF OUTSIDE!"

Amanda muttered several expletives, before dragging herself up to investigate the claim. She rubbed her eyes as she walked, quietly cursing about an array of agitations, her speech ending with:

"...and the worst thing about this whole holiday? I HATE those stupid T-shirts!"

* * *

There were large gaps between the rungs of the ladder. Fleur felt a fresh sense of foreboding each time her foot searched the darkness for the next step. Eric pointed the spotlight towards her from the rooftop, attempting to illuminate the route. The beam had the unfortunate side effect of making its surroundings blacker by comparison. Mosquitoes circled the pink glow, providing little comfort in their confusion.

Fleur breathed a sigh of relief once both trainers had touched the ground.

Stepping away from the wall, she blinked repeatedly to remove the mass of magenta lingering in her vision. Eric gradually came into view. His right hand rode the metal, as his legs effortlessly riverdanced the rungs.

Fleur felt fearful as he approached.

"How was your ankle on the way down?"

"Fine," she replied.

Her eyes did not leave the hotel staff. They quickly retrieved the ladder and folded it up, their practised hands making short work of the task. They scuttled away with the equipment

Chapter Five

tucked into their armpits. Fleur nodded in thanks as they passed. Eric could feel the cold, familiar loneliness creeping in.

"Why won't you look at me?"

His injuries throbbed with fresh intensity. The silence inspired Fleur to meet his gaze. His next question caught her off-guard, "What's your name?"

"Fleur," she answered, after a few seconds of seeming to forget it. "Look, I really want to believe you. I've been in this situation. But I don't know anything about you or your -"

"How did you escape?" Eric interrupted, in his usual cold tone. "The relationship."

A rippling of dread disturbed the air around them. Fleur cleared her throat.

"I flew somewhere he couldn't find me."

A pair of passing holidaymakers distracted her attention. She dutifully straightened her posture.

"Good evening. Well, I suppose it's morning now!"

They took no notice. Her expression returned to one more appropriate for the conversation.

"You promise…" Fleur's hands met Eric's arms. She squeezed. "…You promise me you've never hurt her."

"I promise."

Tethers by Rachael Broadhurst

"If I find out you have -"

He shook his head.

"You won't."

She scanned his face for any trace of deception.

"Okay. Then let me help you."

Chapter Six

Reflections of early morning sunlight rippled through the still-cold water of the swimming pool. Four musicians were beating traditional African drums from a small island, shouting in rhythm when the performance called for it. Eager tourists scouted out plastic loungers - throwing open towels, applying lotions and taking first sips of multicoloured cocktails.

Fleur darted between the chairs, checking in with the guests.

"I'll have a rum and cola, love," an elderly lady requested.

"That's not my job, I'm afraid."

The husband licked his lips.

"Sounds lovely. I'll take one too!"

Fleur let out a defeated sigh. The poolside bar was busy; she joined the queue. One overworked member of staff ran around the small shack, repeating a long order to himself as he operated the pumps and optics.

"You need to get name-brand spirits," the customer complained, gesturing to the upturned bottles. "We're very disappointed you've only got the local stuff."

The barman apologised as he added a drink to the tray. This

particular grievance was a popular one among the hotel's guests, although it seemed petty to Fleur, for whom unlimited access to any free alcohol was nothing short of a miracle.

There was a tap on her shoulder.

The hotel manager's thick Italian accent could be heard before she turned, "Fleur, please come with me."

He began pacing towards the entrance lobby, the speed of his movement causing his hair to gather in a wispy cloud behind his head. Fleur struggled to keep up.

"I was getting drinks for a couple, they weren't for me," she protested her innocence in advance, expecting a stern reminder of the hotel's 'Zero Tolerance' policy.

Once they had reached Fleur's desk, the manager got to work rummaging through the unorganised files.

"There was an incident last night."

"I know," Fleur said, "how's the husband?"

Her boss retrieved an Accident Report.

"I need you to find out. Mr Ryang is still in his room."

Fleur took the form without hesitation. The pilot had occupied her mind all morning, every obligation in the hotel had felt freshly hellish as she was kept from checking on him a little longer.

She was surprised that her manager had not chosen to

Chapter Six

accompany her to the suite. The guidebook clearly stated that sensitive matters should require the presence of a chaperone.

On this occasion, she was grateful for the oversight.

"I'll go now, sir."

***

The door marked '306' was propped open by a large elephant ornament from one of the suite's shelves. Cleaners darted in and out, clutching replacement curtains and fragments of smashed lamp. As Fleur entered the bedchamber, she noticed that the wardrobe had been returned to its original location, and the surrounding floor swept.

Eric was seated on the enormous bed, a vacant look possessing his features as the hotel's doctor stitched his palm. He smiled at the sight of Fleur.

"Hi," she said, oddly nervous as she approached, "how are you?"

Eric glanced at the medic.

"Been better."

Fleur pulled up a chair and wiggled the lid from her biro as she sat.

"Can I have your description of the incident?" it felt standoffish for her to be beginning the line of questioning so abruptly. She softened the request, "...When you're ready."

Tethers by Rachael Broadhurst

Eric's expression intensified.

"I don't want any authorities involved."

"It's okay," she reassured him, "I won't take it any further if you don't want me to."

Eric turned to face the open window. Fleur followed suit, reliving their recent escape. Suddenly lost in thought, she jumped slightly as Eric began his account:

"My wife has always hated Miranda. Two nights ago, I received a text message from the girl, some joke about her job as a flight attendant. I didn't really read it, but my wife did."

He lifted a glass of water from the table and sipped.

"My wife wasn't angry that night, she was sad. A dramatic portrayal of a woman beaten down by her husband's lies. Almost like it makes the scorecards even."

Another sip.

"I knew things could escalate, so I walked her to the hotel courtyard and made sure we sat somewhere visible to others."

"By the karaoke," Fleur recalled seeing the couple.

Eric nodded.

"She told me she was flying home early. It made no sense, I need to pilot the Thursday flight as scheduled. She begged me to join her. She does these things."

Eric resembled a newsreader, listing inconsequential items on

Chapter Six

a broadcast with no emotion. Fleur paraphrased his words onto the page.

"Yesterday morning my wife booked her flight home."

"She's supposed to be leaving today!" Fleur remembered aloud. "Has she left hospital?"

Eric shrugged.

"I haven't heard."

"Did you try calling her?"

"No."

Fleur's eyes returned to the document.

"What happened last night?"

Although she had asked for the details, she did not feel ready to hear them. The doctor patted the laceration with a cloth, the quiet taps providing the only sound in the room until Eric spoke again.

"I don't know where she got the knife. At first it was just threats, accusations, breaking things. My wife has her moments. I tried to block the knife."

Eric looked at his palm.

"Once she saw how badly injured I was, she ran to get help. She knew she had gone too far this time."

The doctor tugged hard to fasten the stitch he had just tied.

Tethers by Rachael Broadhurst

Eric paused his story, gritting his teeth in complaint.

"When she returned from the pharmacy," he continued, "she bandaged me up, as if playing the role of good wife would fix the damage she had done. I told her I'm leaving her."

He shook his head.

"That never ends well."

As Eric recited the events that ensued, Fleur wondered how he was able to maintain his monotony throughout. She watched the violent scene unfold in her head, blinking away tears that stung as they quickly reformed. Eric finished his drink and put down the glass.

"No one called reception. The other guests either couldn't hear us or weren't interested. There's no phone in the bedroom, but I managed to grab the wardrobe and tug as hard as I could with one hand. When it fell, her face changed. She was going to -"

Eric's eyes met Fleur's.

"And that's when you knocked."

The medic stood.

"I'll be downstairs if you need anything," his voice seemed overly sharp for the delicate situation. He turned and walked away, closing the door on a silent room behind him.

Fleur looked at the Accident Report and realised that her writing was far from contained within the designated box.

Chapter Six

Eric's words stretched down the page, growing gradually less legible towards the bottom. She slid the unusable document from her lap. It performed a somersault in the air, before crashing down onto the stone.

"Listen," she wrapped her hands around Eric's, "I don't care about the protocol. I'm helping you find a way out."

Eric's gaze met the paper by his feet. He noticed the curvy quality of Fleur's handwriting, the erratic sizing of the letters and the small circles that replaced dots in her punctuation.

"Fleur, there is no way out."

Chapter Seven

Fleur was not in the mood for Moses' shenanigans. Bony fingers in her lower back pushed her forwards. Moses' hand ceased its pressure only occasionally, in order to adjust Fleur's makeshift blindfold, fashioned earlier from his spare trousers. Fleur breathed through her mouth to avoid the musty smell, wondering when the material was last washed but harbouring no desire to find out the answer.

"No peek, no peek!" Moses giggled.

Fleur was surprised that he had not picked up on her blatant lack of enthusiasm. She assumed that her indifference was lost in translation. He halted her walking with an unpleasantly firm pressing of his palm into her stomach.

"Ta-da!"

Fleur uncovered her eyes, squinting as her vision adjusted to the light.

Seven huge balloons filled the sky overhead. The multitude of pristine colours provided a welcome contrast to the deeply grey afternoon. A brand new harness was suspended from metal wires, and tethered to the ground by a length of rope.

Older, faded equipment floated sheepishly in the distance.

Chapter Seven

"Now we have two flying machine!" Moses was trembling slightly from the excitement. "Two customers fly at one time!"

As his enthusiasm was met with silence, he detected - for the first time - Fleur's apathy.

"Something wrong?"

She didn't answer.

He tried a different approach, "You want fly together?"

* * *

Fleur had expected to feel better during the ascent. She studied the coastline of the neighbouring island, as transparent tides gently chiselled angelic features into silky, white cliff faces, and felt nothing.

A fierce gust hit! Fleur found herself being pulled somewhat sharply into the opposite direction; her stomach churned in protest. She groaned loudly and cuddled her middle, comforting her disturbed organs as a second, stronger wind started up. She began to swing like a pendulum.

The force had also caught Moses, hanging several metres away. He, quite conversely, appeared unfazed by the unpredictable flight. His expression emanated wholesome joy, as his body moved closer to Fleur's, then quickly further away. His shrieks of elation grew louder and quieter, like thrill-seekers on a passing rollercoaster.

Tethers by Rachael Broadhurst

As the air settled a little, so too did Fleur's nausea. The airport came into view. Fleur watched the aeroplane bound for England turning the final corner before the runway. The travel agent's logo on the side of the small craft mirrored the one on her shirt. She wondered whether Caroline was on board as scheduled.

"WHAT DO YOU THINK?" Moses yelled, interrupting her thoughts. "CUSTOMERS FLY TOGETHER!"

He outstretched his hand and Fleur reluctantly took it. She glanced at the ground and noticed that the rope to which she was attached had almost reached its full extension. Further discomfort loomed.

The aeroplane accelerated along the runway and steadily gained speed. It lent back and was scooped up by the dense afternoon air, soaring towards the clouds overhead before disappearing into them completely.

Fleur smiled for the first time that afternoon. Shortly after, she cried out in pain.

* * *

"Syèl La is the capital of São Pedro," Fleur explained, opening the Excursion Guide and pointing her biro at a map. "The beautiful island is only accessible by water. If you book your trip with me, you get a boat and a jeep! We will take you right to the heart of the magical capital."

Chapter Seven

Fleur penned the car's journey as she recited her sales pitch, "Here you can enjoy a champagne on us, and why not sample the local delicacies?"

"How much is the Booze Cruise?" Agent Orange asked, pointing at an advert on the page.

Fleur was thrown off by the interruption, "Oh, it's fifty euros per head."

"It's Saturday today!" Loose Lucy realised. She checked her watch. "The boat's leaving in one hour. Do we have enough time to get ready?"

After some muffled discussion, the hens concurred.

"Five for today's Booze Cruise please," Amanda requested.

Fleur noticed that the young woman was pregnant and questioned to herself the suitability of the selected activity. She soon dismissed the thought, assuming that the party's leader was perfectly aware of the limitations of her own condition.

The familiar graphic appeared on Fleur's laptop screen as the device slowly worked its magic. The printer behind her awoke, dramatically screeching as it printed five impractically large tickets onto their respective A4 pages.

"Hey," Amanda's eyes widened with recognition, "you're the girl from the roof!"

The others broke into loud agreement. Fleur flashed them a

smile, before turning to retrieve the papers. The hens seemed to accept the subject as sensitive with a surprising lack of resistance. Fleur was relieved to meet their silence upon her return to the desk.

"Okay, ladies, the coach will collect you outside reception."

They took the documents, gave their thanks and left. Fleur had not previously noticed that Eric was standing behind them. He watched the young women piggybacking and dancing in the direction of their room.

"It's nice to put a face to an anonymous phone call," he said.

Something occurred to Fleur, "I should have thanked them, for ringing reception last night."

"They'll survive," Eric smiled.

Fleur observed a distinctly uncharacteristic lightheartedness in his demeanour. She reasoned that Caroline's departure had lifted his spirits. He approached.

"I rang the hospital. My wife had minor injuries, but she's okay."

Fleur surveyed her surroundings to ensure that nobody was within earshot.

"What did she say?"

"A nurse took my call," Eric replied, fumbling for something in his jacket pocket, "my wife will be on the plane home now."

Chapter Seven

With a smooth swish of his index and middle finger, he released two rectangular pieces of card. They spiralled their way down onto the table.

"Someone else can have these."

Fleur picked up the tokens and studied them.

"The Asian restaurant? The meal's in ten minutes! I'll never fill the slot."

"Well, I'd look rather daft eating on my own."

"I'll come!"

Fleur felt a pang of regret at her outburst. She avoided eye contact, awaiting the inevitable refusal.

"You know what, Fleur? I think a meal is the least I owe you."

Chapter Eight

Fleur knew that time was pressing. She pulled articles of clothing from the wardrobe for consideration, proceeding to launch into the air items dismissed for various reasons. In her hurry, the usual formality of rehanging had been neglected. A rising tide of mess lapped at her bare heels as the search continued.

Eventually, she slipped into a black dress and colourful leggings, both of which offered the immediate benefit of easy access, without presenting problems of stiff buttonholes or unpredictable zip systems.

A glance at the clock confirmed Fleur's suspicion that she was already late.

Making excellent use of her ability to multitask, she brushed the tangles from her hair, simultaneously hopping into the court shoes that she saved for important meetings. She doused herself in significantly more perfume than the bottle recommended and gave her reflection one last inspection.

***

Eric was waiting by the oversized door of the Asian restaurant. Butterflies in Fleur's stomach stirred at the sight of him. She

Chapter Eight

grew oddly aware of her own walk, her arms not quite moving correctly as she approached. He spotted her.

"Good evening."

Eric's silver suit jacket covered a white, silk shirt. The tie was shiny with metallic stripes, his belt buckle the oversized logo of a designer label. He smelled expensive. Fleur regretted under-dressing.

"Hi."

Eric turned towards the doorway with a pivot of his heel and presented his elbow. Their arms interlinked.

"One thing," he said, "let's not talk about my wife tonight. I need a break from thinking about…"

He avoided the word abuse.

"…the situation."

* * *

Spherical red lanterns hung from the ceiling. The walls were crimson, with white Chinese symbols hand painted at precise intervals. Japanese flute music played softly overhead. Scattered cherry blossoms adorned each dark wood tabletop.

Fleur felt that the clumsy mismatching of Asian cultures only detracted slightly from the impressiveness of the restaurant's theming. It was as though she had stepped into another world. The hotel was a distant memory, even as she dined within its walls.

Eric sat opposite Fleur in the booth. His hair was combed to one side, somewhat successfully concealing the swelling of his eye. As he devoured various starter items from a smattering of small plates, other guests admired the ease with which he was able to use his chopsticks.

Fleur fumbled with the unfamiliar cutlery. She dropped and retrieved the same sushi piece twice, before accepting defeat and using her fingers. The roll proceeded to fall apart on the journey to her mouth, littering the table with rice and seaweed.

"Excuse me!" she stopped a passing waiter. "Can I have a knife and fork?"

Eric smirked down at his dumplings.

"...And a bottle of red!" Fleur promptly added.

She was hopeful that a gentle tipsiness would alleviate her awkwardness. The sparkling water in her glass, although refreshing, was a sorry alternative.

"Giving up on the chopsticks so soon?" Eric teased.

He had immensely enjoyed seeing her struggle in his peripheral vision.

Fleur looked up.

"The thing is, Eric, I'm just *too* good at using them. People were getting jealous."

Chapter Eight

Her sarcasm was a mask, covering a face that she was desperate to save. The staff member returned and filled the empty glasses with a fine rioja wine. He placed the bottle on the table, handed over the replacement cutlery and dashed away.

"So tell me, Fleur," Eric watched her prong prawn toast with a fork, "how does one become a hotel representative?"

She chewed.

"No other job prospects, a desire to swiftly leave the country."

She swallowed.

"Then it's just a short application form."

Eric nodded with mock-understanding.

"It's nice to meet someone who is so passionate about their work."

Fleur leaned in and talked behind her hand, "Between us, my job is rubbish. Being a pilot, now that's excitement!"

"Hmm," Eric considered his answer. "To be honest, if you've seen one cockpit, you've seen them all. Although, some of the buttons light up. That's quite exciting, I suppose."

"You see!" Fleur said, grinning. "You've got everything you could ever want."

Eric's face looked momentarily vacant as he sipped his wine; he shook it off.

Tethers by Rachael Broadhurst

"Where are you from?"

"London. The rough bit," she answered. "You?"

"Surrey," Eric replied, patting his mouth with a napkin. He winced slightly as pain passed through his split lip. "The nice bit."

Fleur bit into a spring roll and quickly realised that it was too hot. She withdrew her fork and blew onto the drooping mouthful. Steam rose from the tendrils of exposed vegetable.

"How did you become a pilot?" she enquired.

Eric gave an empty plate to a waiter.

"One hundred percent self-taught."

There was silence. Fleur's mouth fell open in astonishment. He smiled.

"Eric!" she launched a prawn cracker in his direction. "I actually believed you then."

* * *

Fleur looked up from her empty dessert bowl and spotted a familiar guest.

"See that lady?"

Eric glanced at the tourist towards whom she was un-subtly pointing.

"That lady came to the desk earlier, claiming there were too

Chapter Eight

many narwhal inflatables in the pool."

The wine was catching up with Fleur. She could feel prickles of heat in her chest.

"Apparently narwhals are in fashion - all the kids want one to swim with. I think I overdid it today, I put seventeen out."

Eric was unable to hold back a short laugh.

"To be fair to her, that is a lot."

He gulped his remaining wine, Fleur replenished the glass.

"They're only small!" she protested. "Anyway, I didn't tell you the best part. Her name is…"

Fleur looked suddenly downwards, unable to finish her sentence as she fought to contain her amusement. She breathed deeply and faced Eric again, instantly bursting into giggles upon re-establishing eye contact. The pilot was already chuckling, her enthusiasm was infectious.

"…Her name is Patricia Ness. But on the Complaint Form, she wrote 'P Ness'!"

The pair erupted at once into hysterics, the abbreviated name (and its audible similarity to a certain body part) causing them to lose all the composure not yet stripped away by the rioja.

A fist knocked the table. Fleur turned her head upwards, her vision took a second to catch up. The hotel medic came into focus.

Tethers by Rachael Broadhurst

"Can I have a word?"

Fleur stared for a moment.

"Can it wait?"

"I'd rather talk now."

She sighed with frustration at the interruption.

"I'll come and see you *later*, sir."

The doctor reluctantly agreed, "Make sure you do."

He left. Eric peered over his glass.

"What was that about?"

"Eurgh, it's always the same," Fleur answered, before guzzling the rest of her drink. She exhaled loudly. "Everyone working in this hotel feels like they can bother me any time of day or night."

"Hey, look," Eric gestured to a young boy standing behind her, "one of your friends is here!"

Fleur turned and saw the narwhal tucked under the child's arm. She descended once more into giggles at the sight of the inflatable.

Patricia Ness watched on with fury in her face.

* * *

Fleur's walking was extremely staggered as she and Eric

Chapter Eight

made their way outside. With eyes half-closed, she drifted from left to right, occasionally trotting in one direction more dramatically in order to prevent herself from falling. Eric placed his hands on her upper arms to steady her, she could feel the faint prickle of stitches in his palm. He steered her towards a lounger and carefully lowered her onto it.

Eric dashed to the poolside bar, hurriedly returning with a pint of water. He gave Fleur the drink and wrapped his jacket around her shoulders, before perching on an opposing sunbed.

"Are you a little tipsy perhaps?"

"No!"

Cocooning herself in the silky material of his clothing, Fleur enjoyed the trace of aftershave in the lining. She closed her eyes as her brain rocked inside of her head. The pilot was concerned.

"We should get you to bed."

"You'd love that, wouldn't you?!"

Upon meeting his gaze, Fleur was perturbed by the lack of a positive reaction to her joke. Realising quite how intoxicated she must have appeared, she corrected her posture and made a special effort to hold up her own head.

"Drink that," Eric gestured to the water.

She gulped. Her heavy arm slammed the glass to the ground.

Tethers by Rachael Broadhurst

It hit the stone loudly, inspiring Eric to check if it was broken.

Fleur recalled fragments of her icy first encounter with the pilot, struggling to relate the obnoxious man he had initially seemed to the reality that she now knew. In a moment of unrestrained familiarity, she slid her hand towards his and interlocked their fingers.

"You deserve someone nice."

She was pleased by Eric's acceptance of the contact. He stroked her thumb with his.

"It's not that simple."

"Why not?"

He sighed before quietly replying, "My parents would never allow a div-"

"ALLOW? Eric, you're a GROWN MAN!"

Fleur noticed her own alcohol-induced abruptness and softened her tone, "Surely it's your decision."

"Fleur, if I was divorced, my family would never talk to me again! If I lose her, I lose everything. The house, everything."

"Do you love her?"

The ensuing pause had a profoundly sobering effect on Fleur. Anticipation crept coldly through her stomach as Eric considered his answer.

"No," he finally whispered.

Chapter Eight

She felt a fresh wave of determination.

"I'm getting you out of that relationship."

Eric frowned.

"We said we wouldn't discuss it tonight."

Fleur grunted defeatedly, recalling their earlier agreement.

"Tomorrow at 6am," she planned aloud, "you can meet me at reception. I'll be leading a tour group. We'll have time to talk."

Eric nodded. The suit jacket slipped from Fleur's shoulder. He pulled the garment back into position and fastened a button to hold it in place.

"I wish things were different, Fleur."

He tucked a stray strand of hair behind her ear. She leaned forwards. Their lips softly met.

When Fleur's eyes opened, Eric was visibly surprised. His face hovered in front of hers for a few breathless seconds. He sat suddenly upright, straightening his shirt. Fleur remained in position for a short while, just in case he should return.

Eric shot to his feet and removed a long hair from his trouser leg.

"I think we'd better get back to our rooms."

Fleur did not look up.

"Okay. I'll see you tomorrow."

Tethers by Rachael Broadhurst

Eric offered a palm.

"Let me walk you back."

Fleur gripped tight and relied on his anchorage as she stood, the rioja's hold on her still strong.

"Thanks, but you don't need to come with me. I can see my room from here."

"Understood," Eric smiled, "but you're not leaving my sight until you're inside."

Chapter Nine

The hangover was a dull ache in Fleur's forehead. Its intensity made the hotel entrance lobby stuffier, and every perfectly friendly holidaymaker a little more insufferable. The attendees of her guided tour had begun to congregate in an arc around her desk. She scanned the gaps between them for Eric, feeling both disappointed and relieved by his non-appearance. Her poisoned brain tortured her with flashbacks of her drunken behaviour. She wasn't certain that she could face the pilot in this state.

Fleur's manager, observing the scene from a nearby doorway, tapped his watch in her direction.

"Okay, gang," Fleur judged herself harshly for addressing her audience in this manner, "the tour will begin in five minutes. If you need the loo, please go now."

Several of the guests shuffled towards the communal toilets. Fleur faced the table and set the pile of A4 admission slips down in front of her. She reached for her clipboard.

"Sorry, I seem to have misplaced my ticket," Eric's voice was behind her.

Fleur turned.

"Can I take your name, sir?" she played along with his charade, "I'll check my list."

"It's Mr Ness."

"Ah, yes," she fought the urge to giggle, aware that they were close to other patrons. "First initial P?"

"Actually, it's A, for Alan."

Fleur looked up.

"A Ness?"

A bystander snorted with suppressed laughter. Fleur realised what she had said. She quickly looked down at the clipboard in her hand, smirking at an imaginary list, searching the page for the non-existent name.

"Very good, sir. The tour will be starting shortly."

* * *

"To your right," Fleur projected her voice, gesturing to her left, "we have the island's most infamous roundabout."

Even as she walked backwards, she was moving too quickly. The tourists were struggling to keep up.

"You'll notice there are only two roads leading off from the roundabout and three exits. The third road was never actually completed. Don't take the wrong exit in your hire-cars, guys, it's a sheer drop to the rocks below!"

Chapter Nine

Eric listened intently from the front of the crowd. Fleur could feel beads of sweat trickling into the far corners of her eyes, she blinked away the stinging sensation. The loud, warm wind whipped every exposed leg, blowing uncomfortable sand into the tops of trainers. Fleur shook both feet in turn as she moved.

"Although your fall may be broken by the fifty or so cars that have already made that mistake!"

A few eager holidaymakers ventured to the cliff edge, peering over at the rusty pit of vehicles, before rejoining the herd.

"To your left," Fleur finally stood still and pointed to her right, "is our very own Boa Island market. Now, who here loves shopping?"

Attendees squinted, unable to hear Fleur's words over the bustling town centre. Local women holding huge, circular baskets of fruit shouted their best prices. Teenagers blasted music through oversized stereos. Aged engines of passing jeeps growled along nearby dirt roads.

Fleur yelled the last few words, "YOU HAVE THIRTY MINUTES TO BUY THINGS. DON'T FORGET TO HAGGLE HAGGLE HAGGLE!"

Eric laughed at her corny sign-off as the guests scattered.

"You're a natural."

Fleur kicked a mound of dry grass and watched the resulting

Tethers by Rachael Broadhurst

dust cloud.

"Let's have a chat inside the church."

* * *

"I'm sorry," Fleur's apology echoed as her hand traversed the mountain of beige cushions, stacked next to her on the pew. "I shouldn't have kissed you."

Eric studied the blue-painted archway that surrounded the altar, fumbling in a jacket pocket for change.

"Don't worry about it. Last night was the most fun I've had in a long time."

He dropped a euro into the silver dish at his feet. When their eyes met, she was smiling. Her face changed.

"What are you going to do about Caroline?"

Eric was surprised by the bluntness of the question.

"I suppose we haven't got long," he said, sitting down beside Fleur. "It's difficult. I'm sure you understand. I've tried to leave my situation."

His head fell with the sudden gravity of his thoughts.

"My wife breaks down, it's torture. I feel like I've failed as a husband. I can't help her. I'm supposed to be able to help her!"

He paused.

"I can't just abandon my marriage. My family would never

Chapter Nine

speak to me again, I'd have no one."

"You'd have me," Fleur reassured.

"But you live here."

"Eric, you can always reach me. I'm always on my phone at work!"

He didn't respond. She regretted her light-hearted remark.

"You haven't failed anyone," Fleur swiftly continued, "it's your wife that has failed *you*. And it's not your responsibility to fix her, only she can do that. Do you really think she's going to change?"

There was no reply.

"Look, I didn't think I could leave Daniel either, but one day you realise, there's just no other choice that makes sense. I mean look at you. You don't deserve this."

Eric waited a few pensive seconds before speaking, "I've never even restrained my wife. I want *you* to know that. She uses everything against me. Besides, if I were to accidentally hurt her -"

"See!" Fleur pointed her finger, as if to highlight certain words. "You couldn't live with yourself. If you care about someone, you hate the thought of hurting them."

Eric seemed unconvinced, "It isn't as simple as that."

She raised her eyebrows.

Tethers by Rachael Broadhurst

"Isn't it?"

The huge wooden door of the church creaked open; children's curious expressions appeared and disappeared in the crack.

"OI!" Fleur called, "YOU KNOW YOU'RE BANNED, FATU!"

The gang of youths bolted.

Fleur's volume returned to normal, "Sorry."

"You know what?" Eric straightened his back. "You're one hundred percent right. Caroline hasn't cared about me for years. It sounds terrible to say, but I don't even like her anymore! I have to end this."

Fleur nodded.

"Come to reception later, I have a book you might find -"

"Excuse me?"

Fleur and Eric turned as one to address a male holidaymaker, walking down the aisle towards them.

"It's Alan, isn't it?" he asked.

"Eric," Fleur whispered, "you're Alan."

"Of course I am," Eric said, standing up. "How can I help?"

The man presented a mobile phone, "Is this yours?"

Eric patted his empty trouser pockets. "I suppose it is. Thank you."

Chapter Nine

"It was on the floor outside, Mr Ness. I should mention, there was a girl, she was biting it."

Fleur rose to her feet with fresh frustration.

"FATU!"

Eric took the device.

"Honestly, it's fine. Needs replacing anyway. Thanks again."

The tourist darted towards the exit and made himself scarce. He swung the door shut behind him. It closed heavily, causing the disturbed windows to hum their disdain. The loud crash repeated several times before fading out. Fleur shook her head.

"Last week that kid was drinking mayonnaise from a bottle in the café."

Eric smirked. He stepped forwards and outstretched his arms, inviting Fleur inside. Her hands slid around his waist and met behind his back. She turned her head and rested a cheek on his chest, inhaling deeply the familiar scent, somehow far sweeter now than on their first meeting.

"Let's just stay here forever!" Fleur wished more than anything that they could. "The guests can find their own way back."

Chapter Ten

The entrance lobby was all but deserted; Fleur attributed this to the afternoon quiz, audible from somewhere in the distance. She slumped over her desk, oddly enjoying the hard pillow of paperwork. A pain-relief tablet fizzed at the bottom of her glass.

"Eric," Fleur said, "you're the best hangover cure."

The rotating crystals of the chandelier fired arrows of redirected sunlight at her heavy eyelids, just about preventing their usual post-lunch descent. Fleur's head filled with rare and beautiful optimism. She allowed the sleep to swallow her.

A familiar, cold hand met her arm.

"Excuse me?" Caroline studied Fleur with concern. "Are you feeling okay?"

Eric stood behind his wife, his gaze glued to the floor. Fleur sat up without blinking.

"I'm fine," she replied, making a special effort to breathe normally. "A little under the weather. How can I help?"

Caroline claimed a chair at the table.

"Can you please rebook my flight home for Thursday?"

Chapter Ten

Fleur fired up her laptop.

"Of course."

Caroline leaned in, her face uncomfortably close.

"I couldn't make my flight yesterday, my love. I've been in hospital, only just discharged. Oh, and we're awfully sorry about the other night, it's embarrassing."

"It's fine," Fleur wondered whether her tone was betraying her, "I see these things all the time."

She entered the request and watched the graphic. Caroline tutted.

"I hate to mess you around with these flights. This job must keep you busy?"

Fleur nodded, barely able to hear anything over the sound of her own heartbeats.

"We've visited the island a few times," Caroline scrambled to make conversation, struggling with the pauses. "Eric said you helped him with his hand. Thank you."

Fleur's stomach twisted.

"You're welcome."

Caroline beckoned to her husband, he took a seat. Fleur felt a fluttering of butterflies as her eyes met fleetingly with his. Caroline slipped a wallet from his jacket.

"Eric, can we give her something?"

Tethers by Rachael Broadhurst

"No, please!" Fleur insisted. "That's really not necessary."

"Then let us take you out to dinner. Our treat!"

The printer screeched. Fleur seized the opportunity for escape and spun towards the device. Whispered dialogue continued behind her head.

"You're all booked in!" Fleur reemerged with the document. She passed it over. "There's no charge, you were still on the list. I hope you have a safe flight."

The couple rose to their feet.

"I should hope so too," Caroline laughed, "Eric's flying the plane! Thank you, my love. You're a lifesaver."

* * *

The pharmacy smelled sterile. Glistening, white tiles beneath Fleur's feet comprised the only sand-free surface of the entire ground floor. The meticulous cleaner polished spaces between cough syrups, whistling an improvised melody. Fleur approached.

"Excuse me?"

"Please, no English," the worker replied, tapping his chest with the cloth. "I get doctor."

He disappeared through a doorway. A muffled exchange of sentences in Portuguese ensued from behind the wall. Before long, the medic was pacing in Fleur's direction.

Chapter Ten

"WHERE WERE YOU?" he shouted, his hands landing on her shoulders. "I told you to come and see me last night!"

Fleur took a large step back, dramatically freeing herself.

"What is it?"

"I think you'd better join me in my office, Fleur."

The doctor was already moving. She followed him inside and took her seat. He closed the door before joining her at the table.

"Listen," he tapped his fingers on the wood, "I don't know how you met that man."

"Eric?" Fleur's head tilted. "What about him?"

The medic slid open a drawer and pulled out a yellow folder.

"I was given his wife's Accident Report and photographs."

Fleur was already defensive, "I don't believe a word that woman says."

He spread the papers across the desk.

"These are from five months ago. This isn't their first visit to the hotel."

Fleur glanced at the images and immediately regretted doing so.

"Eric didn't do this."

The doctor pointed his fountain pen nib towards the page and read aloud.

"Six eyewitnesses confirm that Mrs Ryang's partner became violent in the reservation-only restaurant. He was initially seen dining with another woman, leading hotel staff to believe that the incident was jealousy motivated. Caroline lashed out verbally, attracting the attention of several other guests. In retaliation, she was physically assaulted, sustaining minor injuries before staff were able to intervene."

The medic looked up.

"There are six signatures! I saw her later that evening, after he'd made himself scarce. Bruised ribs, a black eye, -"

"PLEASE!" Fleur screamed, her blood boiling; she could feel the heat billowing from her forehead. She stood and turned to leave. "I can't listen to this."

"I know it must be difficult to hear," the doctor spoke to Fleur's back. "Some men are very good manipulators."

She faced him, disgust at his patronisation visible in her expression. He shot to his feet with fresh vigour.

"Fleur, the man is a monster! I don't want to see you in the same condition as her."

"Why didn't you ring the police?" Fleur protested.

"Caroline begged everyone to hush it up. Reputation is everything to that couple."

Fleur was unsure what to do with the information.

Chapter Ten

"Two nights ago," the medic continued, "I saw the same look of terror in her face when she came to the pharmacy for bandages."

"You also saw his injuries!" Fleur snapped. "How do you explain his hand?"

"Listen, I'm not saying Mrs Ryang's an angel. I'm just strongly suggesting that *you* don't get involved in their marriage."

Fleur sensed his good intentions, in spite of his inelegant approach.

"Sir, you honestly don't need to worry about me. I won't be seeing Eric again."

* * *

A very sunburnt couple were waiting outside of the doctor's office, their mouths agape. As Fleur passed, she realised that they had likely heard the entire exchange. She avoided looking in their direction.

Fleur paced towards reception, her confusion warping into disgust, into suffocating sadness. She hoped that none of it showed on her face. Caroline came into view, deep in discussion with the hotel manager.

"Ah, my favourite employee!" Fleur's boss called out. "Can I see you in my office for five?"

It was obvious that he would abandon his relaxed attitude in moments. His friendly persona was seldom present longer than holidaymakers within earshot. Fleur accompanied him into the large room that he had designated to his relatively minor daily tasks. They were seated.

"I have had a report about your behaviour," he said, "were you drinking with a guest last night?"

"Did Caroline tell you that?" Fleur's concern was misplaced. "Why didn't she say anything to me? Just then?"

The manager shook his head.

"It doesn't matter who made the accusation."

Fleur deduced that the information must have come from a different source. She realised that she was not listening.

"...and it just seems as though you're not taking the job seriously."

Fleur made a sudden effort to look remorseful rather than pensive.

"Consider this your final warning!" the boss snapped, sliding a coffee-stained Disciplinary Form along the table. He placed a pencil by its side. "No more drinking with the guests. No more leaving work before your shift ends."

Fleur scrawled her signature.

"I'm really sorry. It won't happen again."

Chapter Eleven

Amanda did not want to leave the hotel. She walked, arms interlinked with Lucy, listening to her friend's overly optimistic predictions about her upcoming date.

"It's just so romantic that Mario wants to take me to the beach."

"This whole island is a beach!" Amanda retorted.

The pair reached the staircase. Lucy's stilettos wobbled with each uncertain step.

"Watch it, you're going too quickly," she complained.

Amanda slowed her descent.

"I told you not to wear those!"

In spite of her multiple reservations, Amanda felt sure that her evening of safe-guarding would prove to be mildly less insufferable than the hotel's bingo event. The rest of the hen party did not share the opinion; they had heard great things about a certain host named Henry and were very much looking forward to meeting the man himself.

"Lucy, are you absolutely sure Mario is safe?" Amanda was already embodying the mother that she was soon to become. "We've only met him once."

Tethers by Rachael Broadhurst

"Well, he spent the night here and didn't kill me."

They approached the hotel representative's desk.

"Oi, Fiddler on the Roof," Lucy addressed Fleur who was busy disassembling her stall.

Amanda sighed, confident that her friend knew nothing of the musical to which she was referring.

"Hey," Amanda noticed Fleur's erratic breathing, "are you alright?"

Fleur could no longer contain her emotion. She sunk into despair, covering her face with both hands. Tears bounced off of the metal framework below. Amanda outstretched her arms welcomingly.

"Hey, you'll be alright."

Fleur instinctively backed away, wiping her eyes with a shirt sleeve and glancing at the resulting makeup smudge on her cuff.

"I'm sorry," she said, before sniffing hard. "It's been a really bad day."

Amanda gestured towards her friend, "I've had a week of dealing with these drunken hoes. I get it."

Fleur smiled through her stifled emotion.

"I'm sorry," she felt the need to apologise again. "How can I help?"

Chapter Eleven

"Can you book us a cab to The Social Club?" Lucy asked, somewhat bluntly given the headspace of the question's recipient.

"Of course."

Fleur sat at the tilting, half-collapsed desk and lifted the landline receiver. The buttons were stiff as she dialled. The equipment clicked, attempting a connection.

"Do you want to leave straight away?" Fleur asked.

She held the phone to her chest as the recorded message played, firmly pressing the keypad at appropriate intervals using only her experience of the timings. The ladies nodded, she hit the number one.

"Hey, my friend's meeting someone tonight," Amanda said. "Why don't you join us? Keep me company. You've just finished your shift, right?"

"That's very nice of you," Fleur replied, "but I'm not allowed. I'm off alcohol for a while anyway."

"I know the feeling," Amanda's hand circled her stomach. "Come on, you'll feel better."

"You can bring your boyfriend," Lucy piped up, recalling the man from the roof. "He's cute!"

Amanda slapped her friend's knees in playful disapproval. Fleur shuddered at the mention of Eric.

"I'll come. I need to get out of this place."

Tethers by Rachael Broadhurst

* * *

It was Reggae Night at The Social Club, Boa Island's premiere beachfront drinking establishment. There was no ceiling, just three rattan walls held up by bamboo shoots staked into the sand. Three musicians performed from a stage area next to the canoe-shaped bar, they were uncomfortably loud in Fleur's ear as she ordered. The venue was brimming with enthusiastic punters, stumbling as they danced on the sand, frequently knocking over and repositioning the knee-high drums with which the floor space was decorated.

Outside, Amanda rocked gently back and forth on a swing, suspended by a rusted-metal frame. She watched the colourful sky fading into darkness over the ocean, favouring the salty sea scent over the alcohol-infused air of the club. Her sense of smell had been particularly sensitive of late. Fleur approached and handed over a glass of lemonade.

"Where's Lucy?"

Amanda pointed. By the waves, two distant silhouettes ran towards one another. Lucy and Mario met, proceeding to entangle themselves in a passionate kiss. Amanda awkwardly averted her eyes.

"Mate, on Friday night, I was stuck in the back of a taxi with that."

She could feel Mario's body heat on her thigh once more. Fleur sipped her coffee-coloured concoction, wincing as the terrible

Chapter Eleven

taste hit her tongue. Amanda glanced in her direction.

"Thought you weren't drinking?"

"Desperate times," Fleur replied between gulps.

There was a round of applause from the revellers as the band finished a number. The ladies joined in. Fleur slapped the drink in her hand until it spilled over the rim.

"You know, we don't get many hen parties on the island."

Amanda wasn't surprised, "The lack of anything to do is a problem."

Their collective vision rejoined Lucy and her lover. They were now barefoot and dancing together. Mario lifted an arm for Lucy to pass under, before leaning forwards and reclining her in his embrace.

"I'm happy being single," Fleur was almost convincing.

"Bad experience? Wanna talk about it?" Amanda was desperate for anything to distract her from the display.

"Very bad," a wave of nausea washed over Fleur as she remembered the images on the doctor's table. "I just can't believe I've made the exact same mistake twice. Why do I always fall for people who are just the absolute worst?"

She withheld the details, "The saddest thing is, I still really want to believe him."

"Well," Amanda shrugged, "what makes you so sure he's

lying?"

Fleur finished her cocktail and crouched down. She spun the stem of the empty glass, burying the base in the sand.

"Six eyewitnesses."

"That is pretty hard to dispute," Amanda quietly agreed.

Lucy and Mario strolled in their direction. There was a scuffling somewhere to Fleur's left as she stood. Patrons swayed from left to right; someone was pushing their way through the crowd. A furious woman emerged. The stomping of her feet left deep imprints in the beach as she approached.

"MARIO!" she managed somehow to shout through gritted teeth. "WHO IS THIS?"

She pointed at Lucy.

"A friend. Nobody!" Mario protested, darting up to his jilted aggressor and attempting a hug. "Julia, please."

"DON'T LIE TO ME!"

Julia shunted his shoulders. Mario fell into the audience, warping the confused back row like plexiglass, before scrambling to his feet.

The woman immediately dived in front of him, screaming, "YOU LYING, CHEATING -"

Mario's fist sunk into her stomach! Onlookers gasped as Julia bowed from the waist.

Chapter Eleven

"I'M NOT A CHEAT!" Mario yelled, being swiftly dragged away and angrily reprimanded by bartenders.

Julia fell sobbing into strangers' arms. She was quickly surrounded by sympathetic tones and sips of soft drinks. She removed a gold ring and threw it. The metal bounced somewhere near the feet of Fleur, for whom movement had become barely possible.

There was a sickness, Fleur felt it manifest as a solid mass in her throat. Her breath was hard to catch, her eyes too dry and tired to cry, though they burned with the desire.

*** * ***

Dear Sarah,
I'm afraid I must write again.
It seems Daniel is still with me, he's waiting
around every corner.

Chapter Twelve

It rained very infrequently on the island. The rare weather was being celebrated by the locals. Children were frantically engaged in water fights; they kicked the warm puddles and launched muddy arcs towards mock nemeses. Elders bathed their feet in small pools, exchanging tales of wet days of old.

Every member of entrance staff was outside, with the exception of Fleur. She sat watching two large drops racing the length of a window behind her desk.

She picked her favourite, it lost.

Her focus shifted to a bellboy on the other side of the glass, laughing as he waltzed with a pregnant street dog. The man held the front paws and swayed. The stray lapped towards the sky, savouring each delicious drip of the shower despite being quite baffled by her own standing on two legs.

Fleur faced away from the morning frivolity, closing her eyes and groaning loudly to drown out the relentless noise of her mind.

The man in front of her was whispering, "Are you okay?"

She paused before allowing herself to look up.

"What do you want, Eric?"

Chapter Twelve

"Caroline's asleep," he took a seat. "We haven't got much time."

He appeared confused by her disinterest but continued, "I've booked a new hotel. I'm moving tomorrow. I'm leaving Caroline, Fleur! I wanted to see you before I go."

He extended both arms and interlocked their fingers. Photographs of injuries flashed through Fleur's mind as she was held by the hands that had caused them. She jerked free of his clutch and shifted back her chair so that he was unable to re-establish it.

"I don't want to see you."

Eric attempted to diagnose her neglect of his situation.

"You're angry because I went back to the room with her yesterday. It doesn't mean anything. Trust me, it was nothing but arguments. My usual hotel was fully booked. I slept on the -"

"Please," desperation possessed Fleur's face and tone at once, "leave me alone."

Eric's eyes widened.

"Why?"

"The medic told me everything. You and Caroline deserve each other."

"What did he -" Eric's sentence changed. "You think I deserve this?"

Tethers by Rachael Broadhurst

Fleur rose to her feet.

"What I think doesn't matter. I can't be involved with you two."

The downpour drummed on the roof, matching in rhythm Fleur's hurried footsteps through the lobby.

Eric paced behind her.

"You need to listen to me."

Fleur spun.

"So you can lie to me again? Manipulate me? This is your final warning, get away from me or I'm calling the police!"

Fleur turned before his expression could inspire sympathy. She marched through the sliding doors. Workers cheered at her appearance in the forecourt, raising their arms as Fleur's face fell.

Rainwater raced her tears to the ground.

***

"Let's get you in your flying gear!" Fleur's forced enthusiasm was so convincing that she almost fell for it herself.

She clipped the harness around the young boy's chest and tugged the strap hard. He jerked forwards with the pull. Fleur took his hand and led him onto the outdoor scales.

"Okay, how many balloons do you need?"

The machinery sank a little into the sand with his small weight.

Chapter Twelve

Moses had penned the conversions onto the outer wall of his concrete office building. Fleur leaned in and squinted at the handwriting, deciphering the required number.

"Three balloons, excellent."

Fleur checked the tightness of the material around the child's middle.

"Three is actually a really exciting number. Do you know that we live on the third planet from the sun? Contrary to popular belief, there are only three primary col-"

"Alexandre doesn't speak much English," a French accent chimed in. The mother's smile juxtaposed the abruptness of her interruption.

Fleur persisted with the cheery façade, "In Greek mythology," she knew the word 'mythology' was an especially ambitious choice, "the Gods ruled over three kingdoms - the underworld, the water and…"

She gestured to the sky, concluding her speech, "…the heavens!"

Alexandre observed Fleur with sheer bewilderment, then managed a half-smile. His pity felt somehow more insulting than his indifference. Huge balloons swayed above their heads. It never ceased to amaze Fleur that rusty hooks in the ground were strong enough to tether the equipment. She released the first carabiner. Rubber bobbed in her direction. Lingering rainwater from the surface peppered the route to

Tethers by Rachael Broadhurst

Alexandre with small showers. Patches of dry earth quickly drank the resulting puddles. Fleur clicked the metal to the boy's back and reached for the next wire.

His mother patted her face with a handkerchief, removing evidence of ongoing splashes. Fleur fixed the second line to the harness.

Alexandre suddenly began to drift upwards!

Fleur quickly wrapped her arms around his waist to halt his ascent. She had forgotten Moses' golden rule: *NEVER attach the balloons before the tether.*

"WHAT ON EARTH?" the mother paced forwards and grounded her boy with a sharp yank of his wrist. "Are you out of your mind, madam?!"

Fleur swiftly secured the rope to Alexandre's chest, as if doing so with sufficient speed would rectify the situation. The panic lingered as a dense fog inside of her head, she could hear her heartbeat somewhere in the middle. Alexandre's mother squeezed her son's shoulders, holding him down while Fleur reached for the third balloon. The child's eyes were wide with fear as it snapped into position.

Fleur built tension in the limited French that she knew, "Trois - deux - UN!"

Alexandre's protector let go. The boy shot up like a rocket! His alarmingly quick ascent continued until the rope was taut moments later. The child's high-pitched yelp of pain was

Chapter Twelve

audible from the ground. Fleur felt her own body ache in sympathy.

"ARE YOU OKAY?" she shouted at the sky.

"Oui," his voice only just reached her.

"Is that normal?" the mother watched on with growing concern. "How do you get him down?"

Fleur glanced at Moses' workers. They cleaned a car, dipping their once-yellow rags in the thick, brown water (doing significantly more harm than good).

"Those guys," she withheld the details of the landing procedure for now, enjoying the inevitably short-lived break from the woman's scorn.

Moses appeared, running with bare feet and pointing at Alexandre.

"ONLY TWO BALLOON! TWO BALLOON!" he yelled, jumping on the spot, "HE IS TINY CHILD! THREE IS TOO MUCH BALLOON!"

Fleur realised quite how illegible the writing on the wall must have been. She had not felt overwhelmingly concerned for Alexandre's welfare prior to Moses' announcement. It was not exactly easy to differentiate between a regulation flight and a disastrous one. Moses was hardly a poster boy for air safety.

"Look, I know you're probably upset," Fleur faced the seething mother. "I'd like to offer your son a complimentary Moses pencil topper from the gift shed."

* * *

The corridors of the hotel were cream in colour, although hanging rectangular lights tinted certain walls amber after four o'clock. Fleur had heard them blinking into action. She snaked through the building. Upon locating the correct room, she hesitated slightly, listening for any indication of life behind the door.

Hearing nothing, she knocked. The handle shifted and Amanda appeared.

"Fleur! How are you doing, mate?"

"Fine, thanks. I thought Lucy may appreciate this," she presented champagne.

The hotel granted their representative one free bottle per week, to donate to a guest of their choice. Fleur had rewarded, thus far, the holidaymakers with whom she had shared the least interaction. After Lucy's disastrous date, however, it was clear that the gesture had a more worthy recipient on this occasion.

"Maybe Lucy needs a break from drinking," Amanda said, turning to look at her friend.

A moat of used tissues surrounded a pillow fort, from which Lucy stared despondently back. Amanda faced Fleur.

Chapter Twelve

"Do you want to come in?"

* * *

"According to the bar staff," Lucy sniffled, "all the locals know about Mario's womanising."

Fleur poured champagne into a flute atop the bed, holding the base as it wobbled with the weight of the liquid. The first sip hurt her teeth a little with its coldness. Amanda stroked Lucy's arm.

"Come on, mate, you barely knew him. You'll find someone else, you always do."

Lucy blinked back the emotion.

"Mario was just so sweet, he said such nice things."

Amanda tutted, "I'm surprised he found the time. He never came up for air!"

Lucy's eyes tightly closed. Tears fell from the corners.

"I'm sorry," Amanda adopted a kinder persona. "I don't know what's wrong with me lately. I'm here for you, Luce. Take as long as you need."

Fleur downed her drink in one gulp.

"These glasses are too small, that's what I know."

"Are you sure you should be drinking?" Amanda's mother instinct enquired.

"It's fine," Fleur replenished the flute. "Tuesday evening is the only free time I get, I might as well enjoy it."

"Good for you," Lucy nodded. "I'm going to join you, let's order more!"

Amanda sighed.

* * *

Fleur steadied herself with a hand on the wall. Her palm glided along the smooth surface as her tangled legs negotiated the corridor. There were footsteps behind her.

"Fleur?"

She rotated her body in one floppy motion to address the voice.

Eric materialised from blur, "Fleur, are you drunk?"

"Why do *you* care?"

With a decisive spin, she faced away and resumed her stumbling.

"I'm walking to the forecourt," he caught her up. "Needed fresh air. Will you join me?"

She gained speed.

"No. And I'll call the police if you keep harassing me."

"Fleur, please don't do that. Just tell me why you're being so dismissive."

Chapter Twelve

"Eurgh," she sensed that he would not give up easily. Her heavy head checked in both directions to ensure that nobody was nearby. "I know what you did to Caroline."

He was speechless for a moment.

"What did I do?"

"Eric, I saw photos of her injuries. You can drop the act."

He shook his head.

"Caroline got her dislocation from the bedroom door. Fleur, you were there!"

"I'm talking about five months ago!" she snapped.

There was a silence as Eric thought back. Fleur swallowed down the rising sickness.

"I saw the Accident Report. SIX witnesses. I suppose they were all lying?"

"I wasn't here five months ago," Eric recalled. "My wife visited the hotel with friends. She was mugged. Were there witnesses?"

Fleur's eyes widened.

"You're telling me criminals beat her up? For what, a handbag?"

"That's what she told me."

"Eric, you need to stop lying!"

Fleur's legs had been growing weaker. The left knee buckled suddenly and she began to drift towards the wall. Eric reached for her shoulders to provide stability.

"GET OFF ME!" she cried.

He quickly let go. It took Fleur a few seconds to refind her footing unassisted. She rubbed her skin, as if cleansing herself of his touch. He watched on defeatedly.

"I don't know what you've heard, Fleur, but I have never lied to you."

"Was it the flight attendant?!" Fleur asked without blinking. "Miranda, isn't it? You told me your wife hates her. Was it Miranda you dined with that night? In the same restaurant we ate in, Eric! Do you know how twisted that is? Do you have no remorse?!"

"Fleur," he blocked her path, "you mustn't jump to conclusions."

"Right now you're stopping me from leaving and telling me what to do," Fleur scoffed, "doesn't look good, does it?"

Eric reluctantly stepped aside.

Chapter Thirteen

The holidaymakers had arrived in their usual hordes for the 'Wednesday, What's On?' meeting, filling the outdoor seating area with their yawning faces and unsubtle groin-scratches. Fleur crossed the stage and approached the microphone.

"Good morning, everyone. Welcome to…" she paused, without smiling, for dramatic tension, felt by no one. "…Boa Island."

There was a cough from an audience member.

"Okay, let's start with some facts. Did you know that Boa is the third largest island in the cluster? Or that the main export is fish?" Fleur hated her script, finding the rhetorical questions to be an especially cringey opener. "Now there are a few serious things I do have to mention. Firstly, pool safety."

A tourist whooped. There was a mumble of laughter.

"When you're walking poolside, please make sure you're wearing your shoes because it can get very slippery. Also, we do not allow diving into…"

Caroline rushed through the aisles, her head turning left to right as she scanned the area in search of someone.

"…um, the water," Fleur continued. "Secondly, internet. Many of you will have noticed that there is very limited connection in the hotel. There is an internet cafe in the town, five minutes walk away."

A grumbling from the crowd ensued.

"Maps are available at my desk. Food is served throughout the day in all restaurants on-site and you do not require a reservation. That is, unless you're visiting -"

Caroline found the man for whom she was looking. It was not Eric, although Fleur felt certain that she recognised him. He greeted Caroline with a kiss. The microphone whined with interference. The pair glanced up at Fleur, who was staring at them with her mouth agape. Caroline quickly covered her face with a palm.

"Sorry," Fleur addressed the audience. "If you want to dine in the Asian restaurant, you'll need to book at reception."

* * *

Fleur sprinted towards the entrance lobby.

"Excuse me, miss," a barman started, "when you're free -"

She flew past him, a forcefield of fast-moving wind shielding her from the end of his request.

Fleur reached her desk, fired up her laptop and cursed at the inevitable slowness. The hotel records appeared.

"Eric," Fleur said his name aloud as she typed, "Ryang."

Chapter Thirteen

She selected 'January' from the drop-down list. Her hands trembled as the machine searched the five month old data. No results.

Fleur changed the name in the first box to Caroline. One result.

She double-clicked the booking. The check in document contained three lady's names, and one man's.

Amanda and her hens approached the desk, there was fury in Lucy's face.

"Fleur, do you *know* who is in the hotel?!"

"Mario Kelly," Fleur had only just learned his surname from the computer screen.

"He's here with some tart!" Lucy exclaimed. "Apparently he's been seeing her for ages."

Fleur was already moving.

"I have to find someone. I'm sorry."

* * *

Suite 306 had golden leaf detailing on the door. The pattern spanned the wood in parallel lines. Fleur had never previously taken the time to study them. She knocked again.

"Excuse me," a previously-sweeping female cleaner approached, "what do you want?"

"I'm looking for a guest. His name is Eric."

"This man," the worker hit the door with the end of her broom, "gone."

Fleur felt her stomach drop.

"Where?"

"New hotel."

The staff member resumed her duties. The walls were closing in on Fleur, growing tighter around her body until they were crushing. She cried out with agony. Her pain echoed through the endless maze of corridors, and burnt her ears with increasing intensity each time the building repeated it back to her.

* * *

Fleur firmly pressed the keypad and listened to the familiar clicks of attempted connection. The large phone book on her desk contained the contact details of every hotel on the island. All but one of the eleven entries had been blacked out with a biro.

The rings sounded.

"Ola. Paradise Hotel."

"Hello," Fleur sat up in her chair, "do you speak English?"

"Yes."

"Excellent. I'm calling from the Boa Island Police Department," the lie fell a little too easily from Fleur's lips. It was a far cry

Chapter Thirteen

from her first stuttering call, made just one hour earlier. "I need you to check your hotel records for a Mr Eric Ryang."

"I'm afraid we're not able to give out guest information, it's our policy."

Fleur had grown used to this objection.

"I understand your concern. As it is a police matter, I'm afraid you are legally obliged to conform with my request. I am happy to give you my badge number."

"It's okay. I'll - I'll check. What was the name again?"

The 'badge number' line had never failed.

"It's Eric..." Fleur proceeded to give his surname letter by letter. "...I'm afraid he's missing."

There was a tapping of fingernails on a computer keyboard.

"Sorry, I haven't checked in anyone of that name for weeks."

The news passed through Fleur's body as a slow, cold shudder.

"Thank you for your cooperation."

Ink smothered the last phone number on the page. A defeated sigh travelled through the phone, the receptionist was clearly invested in the search.

"Miss, have you tried the other islands? We have a sister hotel in São Pedro."

Tethers by Rachael Broadhurst

"The man in question is flying home tomorrow," Fleur reasoned, "I don't think he'd have got on a boat."

"I'm thinking -" the voice trailed off. It returned. "I've seen something! Mr and Mrs Ryang are banned from this hotel since their last visit. It says there were noise complaints, Mr Ryang received medical attention. Staff called authorities, there should be police records?"

Fleur said quietly, "I've been advised not to contact the police."

The receptionist paused.

"I thought *you* were the police?"

Fleur swiftly hung up the phone.

Chapter Fourteen

"Who's next please?"

The line of suitcases rolled in procession as the departing guests took a step forward.

"Good morning. May I see your passport? Did you enjoy your stay?"

The record had been playing on repeat for hours in the entrance lobby. The longer that Fleur sat, the more sickeningly claustrophobic her confinement to the desk felt. Caroline joined the queue. An accompanying bellboy dropped Eric's travelbag into the quickly-growing pile.

Fleur reached for her notebook.

> *Dear Sarah,*
> *This will be my last letter.*
> *I know you will understand.*
> *Only you know my true feelings. At least, I hope you do.*
> *I found out you're flying to Boa Island soon. When you arrive, walk straight through the airport. I'll meet you by the red door.*
> *I pray my previous letters will provide some*

Tethers by Rachael Broadhurst

comfort in the meantime.
Fleur

* * *

Fleur and the bellboy worked together to hoist a large, black case into the coach's hold. As the luggage landed, a faint smashing sound was audible. The bellboy assessed the remaining pile, ensuring that no single item appeared too cumbersome for Fleur to handle alone.

"Okay, I'll tell Cristiano to start the bus."

He paced away.

After sliding in the final bag, Fleur jumped up to reach the large door handle and rode the metal downwards until it slammed shut. She hit the vehicle three times with a flat palm. Cristiano received her signal from the driver's seat.

The engine coughed to life. There was a clunking of gear-selection. Stones crunched under the four huge tyres as they began to turn in the direction of the airport.

* * *

Eric gazed out of his bedroom window. Cobbled Surrey streets made no sound behind the glass. Branches of nearby trees were only just visible over the rooftops; Eric watched them swaying gently in the breeze. A bird hopped along the bark, sending loose leaves tumbling towards the ground. With one

Chapter Fourteen

final bounce, the creature was airborne.

"Here's your stuff."

Caroline was in the doorway.

"Thanks," he avoided looking in her direction. "I'm sorry you had to gather some of my things. I just needed space. If I'd started packing, you'd have only worried -"

"I understand," she handed over the travelbag and wrapped an arm around his waist. "Thank you for waiting for me at the airport. And for driving me home. I knew you wouldn't leave me stranded, even after everything."

Eric did not respond. She added another uncomfortable arm to the embrace and pulled him in more tightly.

"We just need to work harder. We're not perfect, but no marriage is, right?"

"Right," Eric couldn't face the predictable overreaction to a different answer, "let's just enjoy a nice evening."

Sufficiently convinced, Caroline released him.

"How about I treat you to dinner? I feel really bad about things between us lately."

Eric nodded. She left the room. He sat on the bed and picked up his luggage. The lightweight, floppy nature of the material led him to suspect that many of his items had not made it home.

Tethers by Rachael Broadhurst

Unloading the articles of clothing drove the feeling of loss deeper. The only complete suit in the room was the uniform on his back. He stood to hang the salvaged garments.

Eric lifted a rolled-up shirt, it unravelled like a yoyo from the collar and a notepad fell to the floor from inside. He picked up the small book and studied the cover, his thumbs moving in circles on the brown leather.

Caroline yelled from a downstairs room, "IS INDIAN FOOD OKAY?"

"YES!" Eric replied, without thinking.

He turned to the first page.

> *Dear Sarah,*
> *Read in an article that writing letters may help.*
> *Writing things down makes them real.*
> *I wonder how life is treating you as you read this.*
> *That is, if you can ever face reading it. I know it*
> *can be painful to think about the past.*
> *Please keep the letters. It's important to*
> *remember.*
> *Against my better judgement, I moved into*
> *Daniel's dodgy, damp, and just disgusting East*
> *London flat. I'm leaving it less and less. He even*
> *drives me to work.*
> *After shutting out everyone who cares, I'm left*
> *with one person who doesn't.*
> *Hopefully this paper can provide some company*

Chapter Fourteen

for the time being.

I don't know how to sign off.
I can't say I love you right now, not while Daniel
is in the picture.

Eric had seen the handwriting before. He leafed through the notepad, it was filled with Fleur's letters. Caroline travelled up the steps. He instinctively dropped the book to the floor and kicked a rug over the resulting pyramid of paper.

She entered.

"Do you have a preference of restaurant?"

"Any is fine."

Eric resumed hanging his clothing. Caroline smiled.

"I'll book a taxi, my love."

She mocked his ingratitude, "you're welcome!"

"What will I wear?" Eric glanced at his almost-empty bag.

"Oh, I must have left some bits in the hotel," Caroline replied. She rolled her eyes. "There are clothes in the cupboard. Have you even looked?"

* * *

Eric climbed up the stairs in bursts, only able to travel a small distance at a time with Caroline's limp body in his arms. She groaned in drunken complaint, pausing her noise only to hiccup in each resulting quiet moment.

Once inside of their room, Eric rolled her onto the bed.

She settled into comfort before turning her head to face him, blinking in slow motion.

"I love you so much."

"Just get some sleep," Eric pulled the duvet over her, "I'm going to read in my office."

He retrieved Fleur's notebook and left the room, switching off the light behind him.

*　*　*

Dear Sarah,
People always ask the same thing.
"Why do you stay with Daniel?"
I've learned not to expect too much of love. He may be controlling, but he has never been violent towards me. Yes, he hates my friends and family, but so do I sometimes! Cutting them out has been oddly peaceful.
I've been threatening to leave Daniel lately. He's all I have left and I'm pushing him away. Even now, he hasn't given up on me. I guess I'm lucky to have love like that.
What if I never found it again?
Today was actually better. We went for a walk. I

Chapter Fourteen

told him how claustrophobic the flat has been feeling and he's promised we'll get out more. Maybe this can work?

"Fleur," Eric stroked the words on the page. "Who is Sarah? Why didn't you send your letters?"

"ERIC!" Caroline called.

He slowly slid open a drawer in the filing cabinet, ready to plunge the transgression into darkness should the need arise.

There was silence. He turned the page.

Dear Sarah,
I had hoped I wouldn't have to write again.
Something has changed in Daniel. He says I make him worse. I don't know how to stop.

Eric looked up and saw Caroline hunched over in the doorway. A chill travelled through his insides. He let go of the book and kicked closed the cabinet.

"I feel sick," Caroline slurred.

Eric darted towards his wife.

"Let's get you to the bathroom."

Chapter Fifteen

A couple in their twenties approached Fleur's stall, their faces wearing matching expressions of concern. The young lady's hair was navy and a stripe of the same shade was visible in her partner's quiff - he had obviously been feeling adventurous during the dying process.

"Excuse me," he ran his fingers through the blue, blurring it with the blonde, "do we speak to you about lost property?"

"You do."

Fleur straightened her back.

"My fiancé dropped her engagement ring in the sea."

"It wasn't dropped!" his wife-to-be corrected. "It was washed off by a wave. They're really strong today."

The incident was clearly a sore subject. Fleur avoided asking questions, the details were unimportant. In her experience, lost holidaymaker jewellery seldom made a reappearance, stolen either by the current or a greedy fellow-swimmer.

"I'll check Lost Property!"

Fleur smiled and rose to her feet, her forced optimism filling the couple with unfortunate false hope. As she scuffled away,

Chapter Fifteen

the conversation at her desk soon descended into a loud back and forth of blame. Fleur slipped through a huge wooden door by the reception.

Beyond the staffroom, a handwritten sign indicated the location of 'Lodst Propperlty'. Fleur wondered how it was possible to fit so many spelling mistakes into one short phrase. She concluded, contrary to her first impression, that the sign was really rather impressive. Items of neglected clothing hung from rows of parallel metal bars. The floorspace was dotted with black buckets, each filled to the brim with unclaimed traveller trinkets. Fleur knelt and began rummaging through a mass of tangled silver. Familiar aftershave drifted towards her.

"Eric?" she knew that it was impossible.

As Fleur looked up, the burgundy of his blazer brushed the tip of her nose. She scanned through the rest of his formal wear.

Fleur stroked the silver suit jacket in which the pilot had arrived for their meal at the Asian restaurant, a sense of loss turning the room cold around her. She removed the garment from its hanger and checked over her shoulder to ensure the absence of onlookers. Her arms glided into the oversized sleeves. She hugged her legs, wrapped herself up in the material, and fastened the button.

"I'm sorry, Eric," she whispered. Her face rested on her knee, she comforted her cheek with the fabric. "I'm so sorry I didn't believe you."

Tethers by Rachael Broadhurst

***

Fleur reemerged in the lobby, her fingers generously adorned with abandoned rings. Her wide grin soon wore off, the couple were reciting their growing list of complaints to the hotel manager. Fleur joined the discussion.

"Here's everything I found just now!" she was keen to loudly overstate the idea that she had been working during the absence. "Sorry it took so long to dig these out. Are any of them yours?"

"We wondered where you were," the young lady said. She began studying the jewellery, tilting Fleur's hand towards a light source for clarity. "Babe, can you help?"

She delivered a faint elbow to her fiancé's ribs. He joined the search.

The manager loomed behind the pair, squinting at Fleur with lingering uncertainty, his recent disciplinary warning fresh in both of their minds. He started moving.

His suspicious gaze did not leave Fleur for a good portion of the journey back to his office.

***

Moses' exposed skin formed goosebumps each time the revolving fan hit. They disappeared just in time for new ones to rise up on the next oscillation. Wearing only underpants, he stabbed at his short hair with a metal comb, teasing it into a

Chapter Fifteen

half-remembered style. He was too busy rehearsing pleasantries with his reflection to notice Fleur enter his office. She placed her bag into the usual locker.

Moses hummed to himself as he donned a white Hawaiian shirt with mint detailing.

Fleur broke his trance, "Going somewhere?"

He jumped at the sound of her voice, before turning around looking suitably embarrassed.

She couldn't resist a smirk.

"What's all this?"

"I have date," Moses sheepishly replied.

"Today? I thought you were working."

"No, Thursday date."

Fleur scratched her head.

"This seems a little early to be getting ready."

Moses turned to enjoy his reflection once more.

"I try on outfit."

Fleur watched the man who was, without knowing it, her favourite person on the island - albeit by default.

"Who's covering your shift on Thursday, Moses?"

He grinned in her direction, "I pay you extra."

Tethers by Rachael Broadhurst

"No, I can't! Can anyone else work that day?"

"No English," Moses slipped his legs one-by-one into trousers as he spoke, "you need speak customers. Afternoon shift is easy."

"But my friend is coming. Please, Moses! It's really important."

"You bring her here," he negotiated, "but she get no pay from me!"

He tutted at the idea of paying another person, although such a notion had never occurred to Fleur. She considered his offer a moment before nodding, anxious to avoid any further conversation about her friend.

* * *

Caroline groaned as her head left the pillow. She sat up, soothing her forehead with a cool palm.

"What time did we get back last night?"

Eric did not look up from his laptop.

"About nine."

He had stayed in the bed all morning, waiting for isolation before making his next move. Caroline playfully threw her arms around him. Notes of lingering alcohol dominated the air around their embrace. Eric jerked a shoulder, signalling a desire for freedom; she waited a stifling moment before granting it.

Chapter Fifteen

She stood.

"I hope we've got paracetamol. My head feels awful."

Caroline staggered in the direction of the staircase.

Eric listened carefully to her descent as the footsteps grew quieter. Once certain that the coast was clear, he jumped up and darted to his office. He retrieved Fleur's notepad from the drawer.

Checking for signs of Caroline along the route, he hurriedly returned to the bedroom.

> *Dear Sarah,*
> *I can't do this anymore. My worst nightmare has become a daily routine. I can no longer hide the bruises from my colleagues, although nobody says much.*
> *My phone is missing. Would he have taken it? I can't ask for help anyway, he reads every message.*
> *I'm scared for my life and completely alone. I need this to end but where do I start?*
> *Daniel's not meeting me on my lunch break tomorrow. Think I'll pay the library a visit. Maybe I can book a flight somewhere?*

Eric turned the page.

Tethers by Rachael Broadhurst

Dear Sarah,
Daniel found my plane ticket. I don't think I'm going to Africa.

"What are you reading?" Caroline hugged his waist.

"Nothing," Eric closed the book, "just something I found."

"Where?" she asked, taking a step away.

"In the airport, while I was waiting for you," Eric reminded her of his earlier good deed in the hope that it would negate his current bad one. "Did you find the paracetamol?"

Caroline snatched the notepad and flicked through the letters.

"Why did you bring this home?"

He shrugged. Caroline tilted back her head and studied him through the blur of her nose.

"I'll post it to the airport."

She watched for his reaction.

"Okay, great," Eric replied. A bead of sweat tickled his forehead, but he ignored the feeling.

* * *

Tears cascaded down, hitting the carpet and exploding into miniature fountains by Caroline's feet. During his wife's brief absence from the room, Eric had done little but wait for her inevitable return.

Chapter Fifteen

"Who gave you this?!"

She held the book in front of him. He could smell the leather of the cover.

"Nobody."

Caroline threw the pad onto the desk, the pages crumpled with the impact. She moved in, her nose touched Eric's.

"It's a girl's handwriting."

He turned away, muttering, "I have no idea."

"STOP LYING!"

Caroline's palm flew into his cheek! Eric stroked his stinging skin.

"The book appeared in my bag. I haven't done any-"

"WHO IS SHE?!" Caroline screamed.

Eric watched a transition occur in his wife's features; anger was overtaken by heartbreaking desperation.

"Are you in love, Eric? Are you going to leave me?"

His face confirmed the worst. The realisation turned Caroline's short-lived sadness quickly back into rage.

"YOU -" a punch to his stomach, "- CHEATING -" another to his ribs, "- BASTARD!"

The final fist caught Eric's nose, causing a sensation of water filling his nostrils.

Tethers by Rachael Broadhurst

His vision was black.

The next thing that he saw was blood on the soft floor, he realised that it was his own. His head hit the floor. He didn't remember falling down.

"Please," he uttered.

A foot swiftly entered his stomach! He let out a winded groan, curling into a foetal position.

Caroline sobbed, "You're making me crazy!"

Eric propped himself up onto one elbow and paused to allow the resulting lightheadedness to settle.

"You want to hear me say it? FINE," he held his dripping nose, "I'm leaving tonight."

The kick that he was expecting met his face! Dizziness swallowed him. Everything returned to black, there was only pain. It throbbed through his features, pulsing in his tear ducts. Warm liquid passed his lips.

Caroline's steps travelled through the room.

"You don't just get to leave."

She left and closed the door behind her. The key turned in the lock.

Chapter Sixteen

Dear Sarah,
I can barely move. Surprised I can write this letter. I hope it will be my last.
We all must face our darkest moments alone.
Today was rough and I have no one to confide in, Daniel is a monster.
He doesn't realise the Africa flight is today.
There's a taxi rank outside, I'm leaving!
Keep these letters. Read them often. Don't you ever let anyone treat you this way. Not again.
One last thing,
Goodbye, Sarah.

Eric's phone vibrated to life.

"Hello?"

"Mr Ryang, is that you?"

The locksmith recognised the last three digits.

"Yes," Eric said, "thanks for ringing back. It's the bedroom door, impossible to kick open. Are you available?"

"I certainly am! Stuck inside again, are we?" the signal dropped in and out, "...driving near yours now actually. Shall I head over?"

"Please. The front door key is under -"

"I remember. See you shortly."

Eric hung up.

He turned the page.

> *Dear Sarah,*
> *What a shame it is that this beautiful paper is*
> *filled only with my ugliest thoughts.*
> *I'm worried about a lady in the hotel.*
> *The pilot is so reminiscent of Daniel.*

Eric read the final sentence one more time. Dread circled his stomach.

His eyes reluctantly rejoined the crinkled pages.

> *Dear Sarah,*
> *I'm afraid I must write again.*
> *It seems Daniel is still with me, he's waiting*
> *around every corner.*

Loud knocking on the front door made Eric jump. He looked through the window and saw his parents' car parked up on the street outside. The 'Fix-A-Lock' van bobbed along the cobbles and veered into a space. Eric rushed towards the mirror.

Chapter Sixteen

His eyes widened at the sight of his own reflection. His nose had swollen to twice its original width, with shades of brown and yellow colouring the surrounding skin.

"There's a key down here, guys," echoes of the locksmith's voice bounced between the buildings as he lunged towards the usual ceramic pot. A thumping of heels sounded out as Eric's parents jumped backwards in unison, perturbed by the close proximity of the stranger.

The front door creaked open.

"He's in his room," Fix-A-Lock led the trio up the stairs.

There was a clicking of metal-on-metal as he got to work on the keyhole.

Eric talked to the wall, "Is Caroline here?"

"We haven't seen her," his father replied. "Why haven't you been answering our calls?"

Eric considered his answer.

"I'm flying tomorrow and I don't know what I'll be doing upon my return. It's Caroline -"

"There's a man here," his mother interjected, "should we wait until we're alone?"

The lock gave a snap and the heavy wooden door shifted. Mrs Ryang gasped at the sight of Eric. Fix-A-Lock avoided looking in his direction.

Tethers by Rachael Broadhurst

"I'll text you the bill, give me twenty minutes."

He darted away, anxious to escape the situation.

"Who did this to you?" Eric's mother donned her spectacles and let out a second gasp.

"Caroline. It's not the first time, but it will be the last. I'm leaving her."

There was a silence, his father broke it, "I'm afraid it's not an option."

He studied the crimson-spattered carpet at his son's feet.

"We've talked about divorce before. You're aware of our feelings."

Eric picked up his packed travelbag.

"I wasn't asking for permission."

* * *

The nearest hotel to the London airport lacked any character at all. Eric's taste tended towards older buildings, with original features and timeless decoration. He found himself in quite the opposite - hundreds of identical rooms, a shiny acrylic reception and excessively bright overhead lighting. He had been painfully aware of how gruesome his injuries must have looked to the woman working the check in desk.

Eric opened his bag, unfolded his uniform and reached for the first of the plastic hangers offered by the wardrobe. The

Chapter Sixteen

bedroom was suitably charmless - plain white sheets, drawers containing tiny milk portions and hair styling electronics, a large mirror and widescreen television, limited to sixteen channels.

Once Eric's garments had been arranged, he retrieved the final item that he had packed. He found the page and smiled at the sight of Fleur's handwriting.

> *Dear Sarah,*
> *This will be my last letter.*
> *I know you will understand.*
> *Only you know my true feelings. At least, I hope you do.*
> *I found out you're flying to Boa Island soon. When you arrive, walk straight through the airport. I'll meet you by the red door.*
> *I pray my previous letters will provide some comfort in the meantime.*
> *Fleur*

Chapter Seventeen

Eric's fringe was a good amount longer than the regulation allowed. He wore his hair with scattered precision over his face, attempting to cover as much of the bruising as the length could manage. As he paced through the London airport, a flight attendant recognised the uniform.

She scurried towards Eric and matched his speed.

"Mr Ryang! How are you?"

He turned. His eyes scanned the area.

"Miranda, have you seen Caroline?"

Miranda's smile faded, "Jesus, your nose. Are you okay?"

"I'm fine. My wife is due to fly with us but I don't know whether she will."

"I can keep an eye out."

Miranda began to dread everything for which Caroline was infamous - erratic behaviour, repeated calls for assistance and demands of special treatment.

"Eric, is she annoyed at me? I shouldn't have text you last week. I'm sorry!"

Chapter Seventeen

"You've done nothing wrong," his thoughts were elsewhere. "Is someone called Sarah flying with us today?"

"Jesus, Eric, I don't know all the passengers by name!"

"Right, sorry."

Miranda studied his face.

"Promise me you're okay."

He nodded, before saying, "I think I will be."

* * *

Fleur quickly collapsed her desk. She had neglected the usual deconstruction process, impatiently kicking the structure until it had buckled to a satisfactory degree.

"WHERE DO YOU THINK YOU'RE GOING?" her manager's voice boomed through the empty lobby. "YOUR SHIFT ISN'T OVER!"

"It's only ten minutes," Fleur protested as he approached. "Please, there's nobody around, the guests are at lunch. I need to meet my friend."

Her boss reached the table, "Tell me you're joking."

"Please, it's really important."

His nostrils twitched with frustration.

"Fleur, you've worked here less than a month and been nothing but trouble. If you leave this desk, you needn't bother

Tethers by Rachael Broadhurst

coming back!"

*　*　*

The front window of the recently-landed aeroplane was a magnifying glass beneath the scorching African sun. Eric could feel his swollen skin prickling in the heat.

Tourists swarmed out of the craft and onto metal staircase towers, held in place by airport staff. The structures swayed a little with the density of the herd. Flight attendants waved-off passengers and welcomed aboard cleaners.

There was a knock on the cockpit door. Miranda entered.

"Eric, your wife -"

"She was on board," he sensed. "Did you speak to her?"

"I did," Miranda answered, "she wants to meet you at the entrance. So…"

Eric looked up and was greeted by a somewhat-inappropriate mischievous grin.

"…I'm thinking we should enter via the side door. Give her the slip!"

He agreed, "Fine."

A faint cheer sounded from behind the wall. Miranda placed a comforting hand on Eric's shoulder.

"I may have told the other girls. We've come up with a plan to

Chapter Seventeen

get you through the airport without her seeing you!"

Tethers by Rachael Broadhurst

Reunion

Eric had skipped the arrival lounge's queue and now faced a new hurdle. The border control officer's gaze shifted from the pilot's swollen features to his passport photograph, and back again. Curious onlookers whispered behind palms as they waited in line.

Caroline stood in the doorway, awaiting her husband's entrance from the opposite direction. Miranda, escorted by a member of security, approached her. The huge man tapped Caroline on the shoulder.

A firm push to Eric's lower back confirmed that he was allowed to continue. He resumed his fast movement through the building.

Upon reaching the usual tunnel, he spun to observe the scene for one final time. The distant guard was carelessly rummaging through Caroline's handbag. Other tourists watched on in horror, as she loudly and dramatically protested the interrogation.

Miranda gave Eric a thumbs-up. He smirked as he turned. He entered the tunnel and rounded the corner.

Fleur stood by a red door. Eric's breathing stopped completely at the sight of her. She looked up.

"Hi."

Chapter Seventeen

Her legs began to tremble with the sudden nervous weight of standing. She gasped as he came closer, "Your face!"

Eric reached out his arms and Fleur dived into his embrace. She protectively stroked his back.

"I trust you got my letter?"

He nodded.

"One question," it had plagued him, "who is Sarah?"

Fleur was surprised that he did not already know the answer, although it was not entirely obvious. She stepped away from him and their eyes met.

"I'm Sarah!"

There was a short pause.

"Although, I go by Fleur here."

"So," Eric felt the need to clarify, "you were writing to yourself?"

"Yeah. The last letter was to you, but all the others were to me, like a diary. Is that weird?"

"No, Sarah. I don't think so."

She shuddered at his use of her old name.

"Stick to Fleur. It makes me harder to find," she requested. She shook her head, casting out certain thoughts. "Everyone on the island knows me as Fleur. It's a much prettier name, don't you think?"

Tethers by Rachael Broadhurst

Eric smiled, still not quite breathing properly in her presence.

She continued, "I tried to disguise my letter to you as much as possible, just in case, you know, anyone else read it."

Eric reassured her, "You don't need to explain."

An urgency flashed through Fleur's eyes, "Let's get you somewhere safe."

* * *

Once they were inside of Fleur's company jeep, she pushed the handle into the groove, locking the doors around them. They took a few seconds to enjoy the immediate safety. The air was heavy with heat, but neither wound down a window. Fleur started up the engine.

As they pulled away, Eric slipped the brown-leather book from his bag.

"I should give this back to you."

"Thanks, leave it on the seat," Fleur's brow furrowed. "Eric, I owe you a huge apology. I'm so sorry I didn't trust you."

"I understand," he replied, "you can't be too careful."

"I knew you would say that," Fleur exhaled deeply, "but I want to explain. I saw an accident report but it wasn't about you."

She cleared her throat.

"Your wife has been cheating on you, for months now. His

Chapter Seventeen

name is Mario."

She glanced across and was surprised to see that Eric was grinning.

"You know what, Fleur? I really don't care."

"Oh, okay," she whispered, still not over the nerves. "You know, I tried to find you after you left last week. I rang every hotel on the island."

Eric chuckled.

"I think I know what the problem was. I worried about Caroline following me. I checked into the new place as A Ness."

"No you didn't!" Fleur struggled to talk through giggles.

"Honestly, I did! Was amazed when they didn't ask for proof."

Fleur's smile was wide as their collective vision rejoined the road. Their gazes met in a mirror, before quickly averting. As they traversed a hill, helium balloons surfaced like miniature rising suns. Fleur enjoyed the display.

"Nearly there."

Eric's hand landed on top of hers on the steering wheel, the familiar prickling of stitches re-enforcing the enormity of the moment.

"Thank you, Fleur. For everything."

Tethers by Rachael Broadhurst

* * *

The dry-earth drive leading to *Moses' Magical Balloon Experience* was steep. The jeep negotiated the tricky terrain, occasionally losing grip and frantically spinning its tyres in an effort to reclaim it. Confusion contorted Eric's face into more of an expression than he usually managed.

"Where are you taking me?"

The huge sign above the entrance was very poorly painted. Moses had clearly felt a great deal of enthusiasm during the writing of his own name, but the quality of the subsequent words had suffered terribly at the hands of his later indifference. Fleur parked up. She turned the key and the vehicle sputtered its way to silence.

"I may have just lost my job at the hotel."

"Oh," Eric did not know how best to respond, "sorry?"

"No, it's cool. I hated working there."

He was impressed by the extent to which Fleur had taken the bad news in her stride. Both of the 'flying machines' floated in the air directly in front of them.

"What is this place?" Eric eyed the equipment with concern.

"Well, it *was* my part-time job," Fleur removed her safety belt, "but I may have to ask Moses for more hours in light of recent events."

Chapter Seventeen

"You work *here*?" Eric smirked.

"The flights are much safer than you'd think," she replied. "Well, maybe not by your standards."

Eric laughed, despite being quite unsure of what was happening.

"So, is there a plan?"

Fleur eyed Moses' office to their left, aware that getting Eric to this point was - more or less - the extent of her plan.

"Come with me."

She opened the car door and exited, he followed suit. They paced towards the concrete building and were soon inside. Fleur slid the lock into position behind them. She darted to the corner of the room, retrieved a suitcase and straightened up the pink bow on top.

"This is for you," she said, rolling the bag in Eric's direction. "The case is just a spare from Lost Property. You can keep it."

Fleur hoped that the ribbon on the handle hadn't over-hyped the gift (she had been keen to repurpose the expensive-looking decoration since the hen party's departure).

"It's only your clothes in there. Not very exciting."

Eric rummaged through the contents.

"No, this means a lot to me. Really."

Fleur dashed towards her locker and retrieved a knitted

blanket.

"Are you tired?"

There was a knock on the window. She instinctively ducked out of sight. Another knock. Fleur cautiously rose to her feet. She threw the blanket to Eric and mimed covering herself. He lay on the sofa and buried his body beneath the wool.

"Who is it?" Fleur approached the noise. "Can I help?"

"My wife and son want to fly," an American accent piped up. The man's face rippled behind the frosting. "Are you free now?"

"I'm sorry," Fleur replied, "but we're closed!"

"Well, that's very disappointing. The flyer said you were open until -"

The complaint grew less audible with each step away. There was a shouted curse word then the slamming of a car door. Fleur walked towards the Eric-shaped pile of material. He sat up.

"That was tense."

Fleur sank down beside him. He offered the blanket and she joined him inside. He lifted an arm and wrapped it around her.

"Now this," she rested her head on his chest, listening to the familiar, fast heartbeats, "this is everything I want."

Eric pulled her in more tightly.

Chapter Seventeen

They remained in position all afternoon, drifting in and out of beautiful sleep, in perfect safety. The air around Fleur smelled like Eric. She had never been this happy.

Chapter Eighteen

There were no breaks between the clicks of Caroline's heels on the marble. She travelled towards the hotel reception at a surprising pace and skipped the queue.

"Has the pilot checked in?"

She ignored the angry heckling of guests.

"You will have to join the line," the receptionist countered. "It's only fair."

Muttered agreement was audible behind Caroline.

"But it's urgent," her lip quivered, "someone's life may be in danger."

The worker's attitude changed, "What's the situation?"

The spectators hushed in curiosity.

"My husband Eric is missing. He flew the plane from England today," Caroline burst into tears, "I just want to see him again!"

"Oh, you poor thing."

The woman at the desk scoured her computer for information that could help.

"I'm afraid Mr Ryang hasn't checked in."

Chapter Eighteen

The manager appeared from behind a door, tapping a cigarette on its box. Caroline flew in his direction, her composure quickly re-established.

"Have you seen my husband?"

The boss dropped his smoke in surprise.

"Erm," he glanced down, wondering whether it would be inappropriate to lunge for it, "can we talk later?"

"NO WE CAN'T!" she snapped. "Where's the rep?"

He sighed.

"She left."

"I need to talk to her!"

The manager knew that he was unlikely to get his nicotine fix without first assisting Caroline with the search. He checked his watch.

"Fleur will be at her other job now."

"Other job?"

"Some balloon thing, you probably passed it on your way here," he removed a lighter from his pocket and tested it. White sparks fired into the air. "Fleur left the hotel in a hurry, something about meeting a friend."

Caroline moved forwards, filling the space between them.

"Call me a taxi. NOW!"

Tethers by Rachael Broadhurst

* * *

Fleur excitedly clapped her hands and jumped into the air. As her shoes landed, confetti canons of sand fired in all directions.

"I'm so happy you want to do this!"

Eric was feeling increasingly nervous, "And it's definitely not going to kill me?"

Fleur considered the odds.

"I'm about ninety percent sure this isn't going to kill you."

He didn't laugh.

"Our track record is fine," Fleur dashed towards Moses' handwriting on the outdoor wall. "We sometimes do four, five flights a day. *Literally* no one has died."

She beckoned. Eric took a few reluctant steps forward and mounted the scales.

Fleur studied the conversions, "Six balloons."

The face of Alexandre filled her mind.

"Actually, I think five balloons will be a nicer experience, more gentle. You're perfectly safe either way. Look, worst case scenario, I release some balloons from your harness midflight. You'd just float back down! Moses would be annoyed but -"

Eric nodded without blinking, uneasy with the life-threatening

Chapter Eighteen

nature of the upcoming activity.

* * *

Fleur had already started drifting upwards when the workers clipped the last balloon to Eric's back. As his body rose, his stomach dropped with a slight nausea.

"Fleur," he reached for her wrists, "I don't think I like this."

"It's fine," she interlocked their fingers, feeling a little amused to see him in this light. "I'm here with you."

Eric could feel his legs tingling with the absence of anything beneath them. The mud huts shrank between his feet.

"Hey," Fleur inspired him to meet her gaze, "look at me if you're nervous."

He watched the scenery expanding behind her reassuring expression. The pale orange peaks and troughs of desert dunes stretched to the skyline, their total dominance of the view interrupted only by the nearby airport. Eric scanned the line of aeroplanes for the one in which he had recently flown from London.

It wasn't long before a snap sounded from both ropes at once. Eric cried out.

"Are you okay?" Fleur began to panic. "Are you injured?!"

He breathed deeply.

"Caroline -"

Tethers by Rachael Broadhurst

He paused, not appreciating the slight rocking brought on by the evening breeze.

"My stomach is bruised."

Fleur tightened her grip on his hands.

"Do you want to end the flight?"

She pictured the jerky descent and realised how little it would do to soothe his middle.

"I'll be okay," Eric said. He swallowed deeply. "Hey, I think someone's here."

Fleur looked back just in time to see the taxi door opening and Caroline emerging.

"She can't get you up here," Fleur swiftly faced Eric again. "There's nothing to worry about, okay?"

Caroline sprinted, stopping before the cliff edge to study the ropes tethering the pair to the ground. Eric's eyes were wide.

"Can she pull me down?"

"No, it takes three huge men. Even a child is hard work."

Eric watched his wife try and fail to yank him towards her. Realising the futility of her efforts, Caroline stomped towards a nearby shed.

"Please don't talk to her!" Fleur begged.

There was a brief silence.

Chapter Eighteen

"Daniel always managed to talk me into staying, however much I didn't want to. People like them, they find the right words."

Caroline led Moses' workers to the scene. Fleur was growing frantic. She gripped the front of Eric's shirt.

"TALK TO ME! What do you want?"

The men picked up the rope.

Eric's answer surprised her, "I want you, Fleur."

Staff tugged him sharply towards the ground. He groaned. A desperately clinging-on Fleur flailed along in tow.

"DO YOU TRUST ME?" she called.

"YES!"

Another excruciating jerk.

Fleur took the metal clip from Eric's tether in her palm and wrapped her legs around his waist. With a click, he was free of the rope!

He flung his arms around her. Their embrace was the only thing preventing him from flying away with his balloons. Caroline watched on in open-mouthed disbelief. Fleur launched the line, which dropped like a lifeless serpent, twisting with air resistance, before slapping the dry earth at her feet.

Fleur was surprisingly calm, as though her sudden decision

was calculated.

"Eric, whatever you do, don't let go of me."

Her hand gripped the metal at her own waist.

"By the way," she leant forward and he met her kiss, the contact infused with vertigo and bliss. Fleur pulled away slightly and enjoyed the close blur of him. "I want you too!"

Eric already knew what was about to happen. He savoured one more kiss, before nodding in acceptance of his fate.

There was a snap from the carabiner and they were released!

Eric rested his chin on her shoulder as they started slowly to ascend once more. He watched Caroline growing smaller on the land through the dancing tangles of Fleur's hair.

"We're heading West," he noticed. "Where are we going?"

"Hopefully São Pedro!" Fleur laughed into his neck. "Let's find out together."

The End

Printed in Great Britain
by Amazon